"I've hired A[bby] to pick apples."

Jake shrugged as he listened to his mother's voice over the phone. "She's the niece of a friend of mine. She'll live in our guest cottage because her aunt's place is too small and our bunkhouse is full."

Again he shrugged. "Is she taking the semester off to finance her college studies?"

"She's thirty-one years old," laughed his mother. "With a doctorate in psychology. I think school days are the furthest thing from her mind right now."

Jake felt himself stiffen at the word *psychology*. "Why is a psychologist coming here to pick apples?" He heard the harshness in his voice, sensed his mother's hesitation. "Did you import her for Stacey?"

He wouldn't put it past his mom. He knew how worried she was about his daughter. Hell, they were all worried. But the last thing they needed was another psychologist.

"I would never do that without consulting you, Jake. Abby's coming here because she needs a change of pace. Everyone can benefit from a new environment once in a while. And although she'll be working in the orchard, she'll be our guest, so I expect you to welcome her and behave yourself."

"Consider my hand slapped," Jake replied. "But keep her away from Stacey. I don't need any more complications—especially from a shrink who's gone into hiding."

Dear Reader,

When my firstborn son was three, my husband and I moved to New England and planted roots that held firm for many years. Mike and I made lifelong friends and so did our three boys. In Massachusetts we enjoyed both city and country living. And as a wonderful bonus, we experienced magnificent autumns with blazing foliage, crisp morning air and bountiful harvests in the apple orchards.

Visiting those orchards became an annual event. Each year my family in New York City drove north "to see the leaves and go apple shopping." In addition, they came to eat apple pie baked by *moi*. Besides a wide variety of fresh apples, the orchards offered the candy and caramel kind, tarts, pies, cider, pumpkin patches and a petting zoo. A full day's activities for energetic kids and adults. Activities to build family memories.

From my current home in Houston, Texas, where I've enjoyed living in recent years, my heart often looks back to New England. In *The Apple Orchard* I indulged my remembrances as well as my curiosity. Who lives at an apple orchard? What happens when the crowds go home? What else could an orchard be used for? A place to hide? A place to heal? A place to fall in love?

I hope you cheer for Abby and Jake as they struggle to find happiness. And I hope you and your family build wonderful memories to share throughout the years.

Linda Barrett

P.S. I love to hear from readers! You can reach me at www.superauthors.com or at P.O. Box 841934, Houston, TX 77284-1934.

Books by Linda Barrett

HARLEQUIN SUPERROMANCE
971—LOVE, MONEY AND AMANDA SHAW
1001—TRUE-BLUE TEXAN

The Apple Orchard
Linda Barrett

HARLEQUIN®

TORONTO • NEW YORK • LONDON
AMSTERDAM • PARIS • SYDNEY • HAMBURG
STOCKHOLM • ATHENS • TOKYO • MILAN • MADRID
PRAGUE • WARSAW • BUDAPEST • AUCKLAND

ISBN 0-373-71073-9

THE APPLE ORCHARD

Copyright © 2002 by Linda Barrett.

This edition published by arrangement with Harlequin Books S.A.

® and TM are trademarks of the publisher. Trademarks indicated with ® are registered in the United States Patent and Trademark Office, the Canadian Trade Marks Office and in other countries.

Visit us at www.eHarlequin.com

Printed in U.S.A.

To my mother-in-law,
Dee Berkowitz
Who believes that
none of my manuscripts should ever be rejected.

Need I say more?

CHAPTER ONE

SHE LOVED Monday mornings. Psychologist Abby MacKenzie grinned to herself as she tapped the brakes of her late-model Mazda 626. She was five blocks from her office in downtown Los Angeles and could feel her energy escalate at the thought of starting her week. Most folks would probably regard her as certifiable. But she wasn't crazy. She merely loved her job.

The light changed and she accelerated, enjoying the absence of heavy traffic in early August. The clear roads served to make the morning sweeter, and she mentally saluted every working person who'd taken vacation. Summer was still only half over, she reminded herself; there'd be many more days to enjoy the relatively empty streets!

She glanced at the clock, noting she had plenty of time before her first patient was due and confident that the four-story building where she practiced would already be open. Early access was necessary to accommodate the variety of medical specialties

who had offices there, including her own group—
Los Angeles Mental Health Associates.

Abby reached her building and turned her car into
the attached garage, carefully making her way to the
fourth level while her mind jumped to the week
ahead. A week where she could make a difference
in people's lives. Cops, firefighters, secret service,
medical personnel. Those heroes were her patients.

She slipped into her assigned stall, reached for her
briefcase, and got out of the vehicle. Looking toward
the doorway of the building, she felt her grin return.
Five and a half years and she still loved being a part
of the practice.

Walking briskly through the entrance, she noted
the corridor lights were on, as expected. She smiled
with satisfaction and made her way toward her suite.

She selected the appropriate key from her ring and
inserted it into the lock, surprised when the door
swung open almost by itself. Pausing, she called
"hello" but got no reply.

"Odd," she murmured as she pulled the key out
of the door.

With a frown, she walked across the softly lit
waiting room toward her own office. Again, the door
moved easily. With a mixture of curiosity and annoyance, Abby pushed it open all the way. And
stood frozen in place…her eyes locked on the scene
in front of her.

Blood everywhere. She couldn't breathe. Couldn't

move. "No," she whispered, dropping her briefcase from lifeless fingers. *Oh, no… No!* She shook her head in futile denial as the horror pierced her mind, ripped her heart and shattered her world. Slowly, her left hand clamped into a fist and pressed against her stomach as she finally recognized the dead cop on the floor.

Her nine o'clock patient. Tom Conroy. A great guy, with a warm smile, a wife and two young kids. Ten years on the force and now barely recognizable. His department-issued handgun lay against the far wall, and his uniform, protected in plastic, hung on a hanger from the top of her closet door. He wore chinos and a white T-shirt. Not white anymore.

Plastic dropcloths covered her couch and chairs, as well as most of the carpeted floor. But blood covered the plastic. Blood covered her unprotected desk. So much blood. Everywhere.

Abby turned her head inch by inch. Like a grotesque abstract painting, her walls had become a canvas of blood-red patterns on a pale yellow background.

She slowly backed out of the room. Think! She was the daughter of a cop, the sister of two more, and knew enough not to disturb the scene. With shaking hands, she reached for the phone on the reception desk and dialed 911.

"I want…I want to report a suicide," she managed to say between breaths. And then stopped short. "No, no, change that," she said as the truth hit with the force of a bullet. "Officer down," she cried. *His mind was wounded two months ago, and his body died today.* "For God's sake, send some help!"

She gave the address and slammed the receiver into the cradle, tears burning behind her eyes. Officer Tom Conroy couldn't be helped anymore. But he'd come to her...to her!...for help in relieving his pain. She'd had her chance and had blown it in the worst way. She allowed the tears to run down her cheeks as she glanced at the calendar next to the phone.

It was only Monday morning and a lifetime lay ahead.

HE HATED Monday mornings. Dr. Jake Templeton grabbed a clean lab coat from the supply he kept at the farmhouse and tiptoed across the upstairs hall to his daughter's bedroom. The door stood half-open. Betsy, their collie, was lying across the threshold, and Jake bent down to scratch the dog behind the ears. When he straightened, he paused before entering the room, the love he felt for his child hitting him solidly in the chest, as it did every time he looked at her. The love...and the pain. The powerful combination he'd lived with since Claire had died in the accident that had changed all their lives two years ago.

Except for Stacey's night-light, the room was

dark. The sun had not yet tipped the horizon. Made sense at 4:00 a.m. on a midsummer's morning in Massachusetts. What didn't make sense was not seeing his daughter for another week. But he'd learned to live with it. He'd see her again next weekend when he made the hour-and-a-half trip back to the family home from Boston where he practiced at prestigious Mass General Hospital.

He hung the white coat on the doorknob, and making no sound in his rubber-soled shoes, Jake approached the bed and bent down to kiss his nine-year-old.

"I love you, Stace," he whispered.

"Hmm."

Was that a happy sound? Had she moved a fraction closer to him? Or was his imagination working overtime? He closed his eyes, picturing earlier days when an energetic girl danced across the room to jump into his arms and squeal with delight as he tossed her to the ceiling. The image almost choked him. *Don't go there, Jake. Stay in control.* He had to concentrate on *now*. On figuring out a miracle to return the laughter and joy to his daughter. The shrinks had failed, but Jake wouldn't give up. He was a physician, for God's sake, a cardiologist whose patients thought he was a miracle worker. Surely such a man could help his own daughter.

He kissed Stacey again, inhaling the little-girl aroma of baby shampoo and talc, admiring the beautiful profile, and once more, reluctant to leave. But he turned toward the door, retrieved his lab coat and walked downstairs.

In reality, he knew they were lucky—he and Stacey. His daughter lived with a grandma who adored her, an aunt and uncle who treated her as their own, and younger twin-boy cousins who kept her hopping. A terrific family plus about two hundred acres to play on and hundreds of apple trees to climb. His and Stacey's situation could have been worse, much worse. He knew that—in his head. But in his heart...

Hell, he wanted to see Stacey every day.

He really hated Monday mornings.

A half hour later, he steered his Subaru onto the almost-empty Mass Pike, his thoughts focused on the workweek. The commuting time always helped him make the transition from his personal world at the apple orchard to his professional world at the hospital. Compartmentalizing his life was the key to survival. He grunted. *Survival* was the word, all right.

Since he lost Claire, he'd become the wunderkind of the Cardiology Department. Work was therapy. No question about it. He'd pioneered cutting-edge procedures to help patients avoid the risks of open-heart surgery wherever possible. The cardiac surgeons and the older doctors in his own department weren't too happy with him. No one liked change and Jake understood that. But to serve their patients properly, they'd better jump on board and learn the procedures, or get out of his way.

If only these techniques had been available years ago, his grandfather would have been alive today. But the grandpa he loved so fiercely had refused to allow anyone to cut open his chest. "Just give me some pills for the pain, and I'll live with it," he'd said. But he'd died from the clogged arteries instead. And that's when Jake changed his college major from botany to biology and concentrated his energies on getting into medical school.

His brother, Robert, had stuck to agriculture and now he and their mom ran Templeton Orchards, where Stacey lived all week. And for that, Jake was grateful. His work had become a refuge, but how would he have survived the last two years without his family?

The sun's rays bathed Boston in a soft glow as Jake pulled into the hospital's parking lot, all thoughts of family gone. For the next five days, he'd focus entirely on his patients and his research.

The only exception would be his nightly phone call to Stacey. He'd never forget that.

ON MONDAY MORNING, Stacey Templeton stretched full length on her bed, opened her lids halfway, then closed them. She turned on her side and pulled the covers back up over her face. Her stomach hurt. Again. Sometimes it hurt all day. Sometimes it didn't hurt at all. But it always hurt on Monday mornings.

She bent her knees closer to her chest and rubbed her belly with one hand. Rubbing didn't usually help, but she had to do something! She'd been to the doctor about a million times already, and her dad said she had a "clean bill of health." That meant she was okay. But she wasn't okay. She knew it and Daddy knew it. The hardest part about it was that Daddy was a very good doctor, but he didn't know how to make her better. And that was driving him crazy.

She sniffed, reached for a tissue and wiped the tears before they could drench her pillow. She wished she could help him. Her dad. She wished he wouldn't worry about her so much. It wasn't his fault she had stomachaches. Nothing was his fault. It was all *her* fault, but she couldn't tell him that. Because if he knew what had caused the big accident, maybe he wouldn't love her anymore. And then she'd have nobody.

She turned over onto her stomach and scrunched completely under the covers. Maybe he already knew it was her fault and that's why he left her with Grandma all week. Maybe he didn't want her around all the time.

But he always came back!

Yeah, he did. She smiled and thought about Fridays. He came home on Fridays. The best day of the week.

LESS THAN TEN MINUTES after making her emergency call, Abby stood alone in the doorway of the suite watching two police officers walk toward her. She hadn't gone back into her office since she'd found her patient lying there, but avoidance didn't help her nausea. None of her colleagues had arrived yet—Abby was always the earliest. But she glanced at her watch for at least the hundredth time, needing the support and companionship they would have provided.

Now she had other companions.

"Are you the one who made the call?" asked the taller officer.

Abby nodded.

"The dispatcher couldn't figure it out. What happened?"

"Combine a Code–30 with a 10-56 and call him Officer Tom Conroy," she said, tilting back her head to meet the policeman's gaze.

The cops stared at her. She saw their eyes widen, then narrow as her meaning penetrated. She'd used the codes for an officer needing help and for a suicide. The identical protective walls that slipped over the two policemen were so clear to Abby's trained eye that they were as tangible to her as the shields worn by twelfth-century knights. Although she often cursed that almighty control that prevented so many of her highly stressed patients from making progress, today Abby could have used a shield of her own to get through the next few hours.

She led them to her office and stepped aside as they surveyed the scene.

"Holy Toledo," whispered one.

"Holy shit!" whispered the other simultaneously.

The cops' reactions said it all, but Abby knew more was coming as soon as she turned around and saw three additional officers, two newspaper reporters and...her dad. His blue Irish eyes were not smiling.

What was he doing here? He worked out of the West Division while her office was located in Central.

"I was in the car when the call came through and recognized your address. I'm damn glad I heard it, Abby. What happened? Who is it?" Lieutenant Patrick MacKenzie's voice reflected his dismay. He patted Abby's shoulder and walked to the threshold of her office where he flinched and said nothing. His eyes widened, then narrowed, as he methodically examined the room.

"And there it is," he mumbled under his breath.

"There what is?" asked Abby in a whisper.

"The note," replied her father, walking into her office. He put on a pair of plastic gloves and took something from her desk. An envelope.

"I don't think it is, but we'll treat this area as a crime scene for now," he said, looking over his shoulder at his associates, "so get a forensics detective and call the medical examiner. Don't touch the body or anything else in the room." He turned back to Abby. "What happened?" he asked again, still holding the envelope.

She shook her head. Her lips trembled. "I found him just like that."

"I know, Abby. I know *that*. But what *really* happened? He was your patient, wasn't he?" *So why did he kill himself?*

Abby heard the unasked question as loudly as if it were accompanied by a full symphonic orchestra, and suddenly her control snapped. She jumped to her feet.

"You want an easy answer, Dad? Well, it doesn't exist. Tom Conroy was a good cop. Ten-year veteran. And two months ago he accidentally killed a child while trying to maintain order in a violent situation on the street. He couldn't get past it. Do you ever think what that does to a person's mind? What happens when the control that you're all so proud of slips? Where was the support from his friends? Where was the support from his commanding officer? You know what happens. Everybody turns the other way. When a cop kills, everybody avoids him…afraid it could just as easily have been one of them! As if what happened to Tom is catching. He felt alone—'' she choked on the words ''—except… except… God help him…except for me. And I let him down!''

The tears fell then, she couldn't catch her breath. Anger, guilt, grief, frustration. She grabbed the back of a chair and held on.

''Abby, Abby, my beautiful girl.'' Her dad's voice floated to her. ''You always did think you could fix the world.''

She felt Patrick's arm around her, felt his hug, and was touched. She wanted to crawl into his lap and be five years old again. Instead, she shook her head. ''No, Dad. Not the world. Only one human being at a time.''

The look in his eye had her chin wobbling again. Pride, wonder. And then, ''The day's not over, Abigail. There's more ahead starting with this.'' Holding it by the corner, Patrick held out an envelope, various size red polka dots scattered all over it. But the blood was dry now.

''Put on the plastic gloves, baby,'' he said, handing her his own pair, ''and read it.''

Her shaky hands fumbled with the seal. She should have expected a note. Should have looked for it. What could Tom Conroy say to her in death that he hadn't confided to her in life? She scanned the page.

I can't forget the little boy's face. I can't look at my own kids without seeing him. My job was to protect people, and instead I killed the most innocent of them. I can't forgive myself. Worst of all, what will my kids think of me when they're old enough to know I killed a child? I can't sleep and I can't eat. I'm afraid I'll jeopardize my partner and someone else might die. So it's better this way. Dr. Mac-Kenzie, you're a good therapist and a good person. Don't blame yourself. No one can help me. But please explain to my wife. You're the only one who understands.

Abby felt tears forming again. The cop's pain was reflected in every sentence. How could she explain to his wife? As if any explanation would satisfy a young woman who loved her husband.

"You can accompany the police, Abby, when they inform Mrs. Conroy," said her father, reading over her shoulder. "But you'll all have to move quickly. The newshounds are here. Forensics will have a report in an hour. We won't release Officer Conroy's name yet, but his wife needs to know ASAP. This won't be kept secret very long."

Abby nodded slowly. "The officers should be from his own division."

"I'll go along, too," Patrick said immediately.

"He wasn't one of yours, Dad."

"But you are." Patrick's gruff voice was betrayed

by his kiss on her forehead, and this time Abby leaned into him, hugging him hard around the waist with both arms.

"Thanks, Dad, but I can do it on my own. It's my responsibility." She blinked back her tears and met her father's gaze.

"Always were too independent," he growled. "Let's see if we can arouse Conroy's supervisor."

TWENTY MINUTES LATER—on her way to meet the officers from the Central Division—Abby glanced into her office. Forensics had done their job lifting fingerprints from everywhere and everything in the room. Tom Conroy had been taken to the morgue, his uniform and revolver with him. All the plastic drop cloths had been picked up. Fresh paint would soon cover the spattered walls, but Abby knew the office would never be the same to her.

On impulse, she entered the room. Crossing to her file cabinet, she pulled Tom Conroy's folder and tucked it under her arm. The details of each of his visits were inside, as reported in her own words, based on her conversations, observations and conclusions. Somewhere inside would also be the warning. The warning she'd missed. She needed time to search. And she couldn't do it in the office.

Her co-workers had started arriving just when the police were removing the body and belongings, and each one's vocal reaction to the tragedy quickly seared itself into Abby's memory. High- or low-pitched exclamations of horror followed by quieter questions and glances toward her. Brief glances before they turned to their own concerns.

As Abby turned toward the exit, her own supervisor approached. Tall and lanky, his wavy hair more gray than brown, Dr. Martin Bernstein was a psychiatrist with years of experience in the mental health field. He was both intelligent and compassionate, and Abby felt lucky to be part of his group practice.

"Don't worry about your other patients, Abby. We're calling them to reschedule, and you're going to take the rest of the day off to decompress...with one exception."

She raised her eyebrow in inquiry.

"When the cops bring you back here, you'll come see me and we'll talk. You've been through trauma today and can use some counseling, too." His voice was kind, not condemning, and Abby managed a small smile. "I'll drive you home later if necessary. Your car will be fine in the garage."

"Thanks," she said, renewed dread filling her at the thought of the upcoming interview with Mrs. Conroy, but she forced another smile. "I'll be okay," she said. "I can handle it."

"I know you can, but this has not been a run-of-the-mill-type day so far. Humor me. Get yourself back to the office after seeing Mrs. Conroy."

"Yes, boss."

But two hours later, Abby knew she couldn't return to the practice that day. Not with Mrs. Conroy's accusations ringing in her ears, not with the woman's ravaged face etched in her mind, not with the confused face of a little boy and an adorable toddler fearfully clinging to her mother's leg still in her memory. No, she couldn't go back to her office, so she had the lieutenant drop her off right next to her car in the garage. Her getaway car.

She got behind the wheel, looked over her shoulder and reversed as though the demons of hell were after her. *What kind of a psychologist are you?* Michelle Conroy's voice, edged with disbelief and pain, echoed in her mind. *He went to you for help. I had to beg him to see a shrink. He didn't want to at first, but I begged him. And now this! Maybe he was right. He didn't want anybody to know. And now everybody will know. The whole damn LAPD will know.*

The lieutenant who had accompanied Abby to the Conroy home was as much use as a wooden soldier. His partner was no better. They drove in silence, not offering a word of comfort. Not one. And now Abby couldn't stop the tears from streaming down her cheeks as she drove from the parking garage. There were no winners in this situation. Not one silver lining in the black cloud.

At the Conroy home, she'd finally gotten one of

the neighbors to come in. The woman had called Michelle Conroy's mother. And Abby felt her own presence was more harmful than helpful by then. It was obvious Mrs. Conroy couldn't stand the sight of her.

She clasped the steering wheel with both hands, consciously counting each street she passed, one by one until she reached the freeway. "Drive onto the freeway," she whispered. Halfway home now. Only one more exit. Around the ramp. A mile up the road. Right turn into her apartment complex. Safely into her spot. Shift into Park. Turn off the ignition.

She slumped over the wheel, her forehead resting on it. A bead of perspiration slid down her back, and she shivered in the quickly warming car. Summer in L.A. heated a closed vehicle in no time. But the heat felt good to her trembling body.

She lifted her head and breathed deeply. Then grabbed Officer Conroy's file and walked into her condo. Locking the door, she glanced at her watch. Two o'clock! Later than she'd thought. She called Dr. Bernstein and told him she'd see him in the morning. He wasn't too happy with her, but Abby didn't care at the moment. She needed time. Time to study Conroy's file. She removed the contents to her kitchen table and began to read.

Her afternoon was just beginning.

ABBY READ HER NOTES carefully, barely moving a muscle, and ignoring the constant ringing of the phone as she sat at her kitchen table. She dissected every word, every phrase, every sentence she'd written about Tom Conroy. Some sessions had been taped. She had the transcripts, but she played the cassettes and listened for voice inflections, nuances of speech.

She felt like a detective. Officer Conroy had presented the classic symptoms of post-traumatic stress disorder: flashbacks to the gunshot, dreams of the shooting, loss of interest in his usual social activities, trouble falling asleep, trouble concentrating. She had urged him to join a support group that she ran, but he'd nixed that.

What had she missed? She held her notes as she paced the floor, trying to get the stiffness out of her muscles after three hours of sitting. He'd kept his appointments with her faithfully, so he'd obviously wanted to get better. She'd had Dr. Bernstein prescribe an antidepressant. She'd taught her patient relaxation techniques.

And still…she'd failed.

She had to find something she'd missed and learn from it. She had to! Because if she didn't, God help her, she might make the same mistake again and…and…lose someone else.

She started to shake. Her well-read notes dropped to the floor. Suddenly, a crystal-clear snapshot of Tom Conroy lying on the floor of her office embedded itself in her mind. Her once-pristine environment, reserved for healing, had been forever marked by her failure.

Marked in blood.

She practically crawled to the bathroom. "OhmygodOhmygodOhmygod," she moaned as she doubled up over the basin and vomited.

The phone shrilled again and Abby picked it up on the fourth ring.

"How are you, dear?" Abby recognized her mother's voice.

"I'm handling it the best I can."

"How about coming home tonight? Sleeping over here?"

Tempting. Very tempting. But she was a grown woman now, a professional, and tomorrow was a workday.

"Thanks, Mom. But I'm fine."

"Are you sure?"

Not really. "I'll be fine. Don't worry."

She hung up and gathered Tom Conroy's file. She placed it neatly on the table, then walked slowly into her bedroom and changed into her nightgown. It wasn't dark yet on this midsummer's day, and she could still hear children's voices outside. But her bed looked too inviting to ignore as exhaustion overwhelmed her. She glanced at her watch as her head hit the pillow. Eight o'clock on a day that refused to end.

Mondays would never be the same.

CHAPTER TWO

TWO HOURS' SLEEP. That's all she'd gotten last night. From eight to ten she'd slept soundly, but after that she'd paced until the soles of her feet burned. And now, on Tuesday morning, she looked as ravaged as she felt.

Abby studied herself in the bathroom mirror, makeup in hand. She had to report to work today; patients were scheduled. They expected to see their therapist as she normally was…competent, smiling and ready to work with them.

She carefully applied foundation around her eyes, covering circles almost as dark as her irises. Her dad used to refer to her as the new Susan Hayward, and even insisted she watch several of the actress's classic movies with him. No hardship. But the only features they really had in common were the brown eyes and thick auburn hair.

She reached for the blush and applied color to her washed-out complexion. Maybe if she looked normal, she'd feel normal. Brush that color in. Accent those cheekbones. Good. No, no. Too much. A clown's face looked at her from the mirror. Blot some off. Even it out.

With fingers trembling, she lowered her hand to the ledge of the sink and held tight. Then took a deep breath. Then another. In—Out—Relax. In—Out—Relax. Better. She reached for her lipstick and twisted the tube until the brick-red color extended beyond the ridge. She started to raise it to her mouth, but her eyes locked on the red color, and her hand paused in midair. The walls of her office suddenly appeared...covered in blood. The splatters, the spots. Connect the red dots.

Take control, Abby! Don't go there. Take control. Now!

She blinked rapidly, rested both hands on the sink and bent her head. Again, she took deep breaths and managed to straighten up. If she were a layperson, she might need professional help. But being a therapist herself, she understood what was happening, and she'd tough it out. She'd control it.

She walked into the front of the apartment, grabbed her purse and Officer Conroy's file, and laughed at herself. What irony! The expert in post-traumatic stress disorder had just experienced her first flashback.

"IT'S NOT WORKING, Abby."

Abby sat across from Martin Bernstein in his office on the Friday afternoon of what she called "the week that wouldn't end." It had been a week of sleepless nights, a week of taking aspirin in the hope she'd be able to sleep, a week of newspaper articles about Officer Conroy, a week of patients canceling their appointments and not rescheduling. She winced thinking of her reduced caseload, not for her own sake, but for the sake of her patients. They needed support and she hoped they had sought out other therapists.

Now Abby forced herself to meet Martin's gaze. She knew what he meant, but didn't want to hear it in words.

"What's not working?" she asked in a carefully neutral tone.

"You."

"Me? I've been seeing patients every day! You know I'm using the conference room until my office is cleaned up. So of course, I'm working." It was the truth as far as it went, she thought.

She heard him sigh. Saw his shoulders slump.

"You're an excellent therapist, Abby. Very talented. I'd recommend my own mother to see you if she had a problem. But not right now." He paused and raised his eyebrows.

"By next week I'll be back to myself," she protested.

"By next week you'll collapse if you don't get any sleep. You're so pale, you look like a ghost.

You cannot go on this way. As I said before, it's not working.''

She'd been on Martin's staff for almost six years and knew him well, well enough to know that he'd just used his bottom-line voice. She also knew what he meant, but she wouldn't go down without a fight.

''I'm sane enough not to take responsibility for *everything* that's happened, for the story making local headlines, or for it being followed up almost every day in the broadcast news.''

''Responsibility? Who's talking about responsibility? You've taken on too much as it is. Every news article is a stab in your heart. And you, my dear, have a tender heart. It can't take too much more of this.''

She blinked back her tears. He'd made a valid point. Worse than the news stories with her name in them were the commiserating looks from her peers, the other psychologists in the practice. Mixed with their sympathy was their heartfelt relief that it was Abby's patient and not theirs who'd rocked the world. They'd pat her shoulder. ''How're you holding up, Abby?'' they'd ask before quickly going on their way.

Even psychologists had to protect their own mental health. Much the way the cops did when one of their own was in trouble. Abby sensed it and understood it. The need to survive came first above all other needs.

"Why did you attend the funeral yesterday, Abby?"

She startled. She'd been so lost in her thoughts that the question came from nowhere. How had Martin known she'd attended?

"I went out of respect for Officer Conroy."

"Really?"

She squirmed. "Yes."

"What were you looking for?"

Now she rose from her chair and started to pace. "What do you mean?"

"You weren't invited. His widow doesn't want to speak with you. Why did you go?"

His words were true. "I went with my dad."

"I didn't ask that."

Suddenly her blood raced and she lashed out. "Why was it so bad to go?" she shouted. "I needed to go. I needed to see him put to rest. God almighty, let *him* rest in peace. Let *me* find peace. I need closure on this!" Martin knew how to hit a nerve, get a reaction. Knew how to prod a person into looking more deeply inside so they could see themselves better. That's what made him an excellent therapist.

She held on to the back of her chair and faced her mentor. "I need closure on this," she repeated more calmly. "And I'm not getting it. I can't put Tom Conroy out of my mind. Because I must have missed something." Her voice dissolved into a whisper as she was barely able to move her lips. "He died because of me."

She turned toward Martin, feeling the strain in her face, shoulders and arms, wanting to sink through the floor and disappear. Guilt choked her.

"Don't take so much credit," Martin answered quietly as he leaned back in his chair. "He died because of himself."

Incredulous, Abby could only stare at the man. "Are you blaming the victim?"

"Let's not blame the hardworking therapist who thinks she has to perform miracles, the hardworking therapist who's becoming a victim herself. All because she's blaming herself."

She took a breath before replying. "I'm not the only one blaming me. What about my canceled patients and Tom Conroy's wife and the...?"

He waved her protestations away. "All temporary and to be expected. Things will get back to normal and so will you—in time."

He paused and she waited, not daring to breathe.

"You don't find closure at a funeral, Abby. You find it in here and in here," he said, pointing to his forehead and his heart.

He was right and she knew it. Of course, she knew it. Didn't want to admit it because the journeys to those two places were difficult. Very difficult to navigate.

"You need to get some counseling, Abby. You've

been through a rough experience and it's not over."
He paused, then continued. "Not with me or with
anyone in our group. I can recommend you to someone else."

"I'll consider it," she replied, "but not yet. Give
me another week and I'll get back to you."

"No more than that, Abby. Your patients deserve
your full concentration and they're not getting it
right now."

Sudden tears filled her eyes, and she let them fall.
He was right. And he couldn't have made his point
more effectively.

She closed her eyes and took a deep breath. "I
have another idea," she said. "Let me get away for
a while. A change of scene. Maybe two weeks."

"Am I hearing correctly?" asked Martin with a
smile. "The workaholic member of the team is asking for a vacation? Have you ever taken more than
long weekends since you started with us?"

Abby shook her head.

"And before that you worked your way through
college and grad school while carrying a full course-
load and getting A's." Martin drummed his fingers
on the desk.

"I took all kinds of jobs," she replied. "I needed
the money."

"You may have come up with a good plan, Abby.
Sometimes getting away can be the best therapy of
all, giving the mind time to heal. But two weeks

probably won't be long enough." He paused, his hands steepled in front of him. "What I think," he continued, "is that you've earned more than a vacation. You deserve a sabbatical. Give your mind a total rest. Shall we say…three months, with weekly phone calls to me just as a check. And we'll see how it goes."

"Three months?" She couldn't keep the shock from her voice. Three months was an eternity. "Are you firing me, Martin?"

"Firing you? Of course not!" Martin exclaimed, genuine concern written on his face. "You're a valuable team member, Abby, but you've been through hell. And now you've got a choice to make. Either you get intensive counseling immediately, or combine a sabbatical with regular calls to me."

Abby's mind raced, but her mouth stayed silent. She'd never seen Martin without his cool, professional demeanor. And his lecture didn't seem finished.

"You know, Abby, the more I think about it, the more I like your idea. You need a change of scene. Meet new people. Find new routines or no routines for a while."

Her idea? All she had suggested was a normal two-week vacation!

"In fact," he continued, "I'll make it a *paid* sabbatical. There's nothing wrong with you, Abby. And I want you back. The guilt, the grief, the feeling of failure. They're all understandable under the circumstances. I can tell you, however, after examining his records, that the only emotion you're legitimately entitled to feel is grief over the loss of a good man. You missed nothing in the file.''

She didn't reply.

"You don't believe me. Do you?"

She shook her head.

"Well, the choice is yours," he said. "But coming in here every day, pretending everything's fine, won't work." He looked her in the eye. "So what's it going to be?"

The words wouldn't come. She rose from her chair and had reached the door before she was able to compose herself. She forced herself to smile and turned toward Martin. "I guess," she said, "I'll see you in three months."

TEN DAYS LATER, Abby took a northern route out of Los Angeles and headed to Yellowstone National Park in Wyoming, the first leg of her journey to the East Coast. The hazy days of mid-August had prompted the choice of a northern drive. She could have opted for Europe or a Club Med vacation, but neither appealed to her at the moment. The open road, however, did.

She wasn't actually going on a vacation, she'd explained to her parents. It was more like an R&R— rest and recovery. And of course, she'd be fine driv-

ing alone. She was an excellent driver and a visit to
Aunt Maureen in Massachusetts was long overdue.
Her mom's sister would be delighted to see her.

She'd done some quick talking to reassure her
concerned parents. Her dad had issued a litany of
warnings and safety tips to her before glaring at her
mother. "She's your daughter, Doris. You talk to
her. Why does she need to run around the country
by herself?"

Her mom had rounded on him. "She's her fa-
ther's daughter. Strong-minded and softhearted."
Then Doris had kissed her husband. And darn, if
Abby hadn't seen her dad blush.

Abby smiled at the memory. Yes, they loved her.
And maybe as parents they couldn't help being concerned, but the truth was, Abby needed to get away.
She needed to see new sights, hear new sounds and
meet new people without having any commitments
or responsibilities to them.

Her Aunt Maureen had provided the perfect excuse to head toward the Atlantic. Although they
spoke to each other often by phone, the families had
had few opportunities to visit. Maureen had spent a
lifetime outside of Boston. Now widowed, she lived
alone in a retirement community, socializing with
her friends.

Abby hummed along with the radio, content that
her plans had fallen into place so smoothly. Even
today, her timing was perfect. She pulled into Yel-

lowstone just as her stomach started growling for lunch, and quickly found an appealing restaurant. She parked her car and entered the building, instantly appreciating the casual atmosphere and rustic decor. Eating her hamburger, she realized that the trip was already providing the relief she needed. For the first time in two weeks, she actually felt hungry.

As she ate, she visualized her upcoming trip. The Black Hills of South Dakota, a county fair in Iowa, maybe a short cruise on the Mississippi, and a little shopping in Chicago. She had no fixed schedule—a unique experience which nagged at her from time to time. Her aunt expected her in about two weeks, but no hard date had been set.

Abby smiled as the friendly waitress brought over her check. She'd already learned the young woman was in her third year of college and had worked the park gig for the last two summers.

"Well, look what's comin' in, and we're so short-handed today," the waitress said.

Abby turned toward the picture window to see two charter buses pull alongside the restaurant. She scanned the room. It was large enough to accommodate a hundred people or so, but young Jenny was right. There were only three servers for the entire restaurant. If those buses carried a full complement of passengers, Jenny and her small crew were in for a challenge.

"I'd better put my roller skates on," laughed the waitress.

Abby paid her bill, started toward the door, but couldn't beat the crowd coming in. Happy, laughing and in high spirits, these visitors to Yellowstone were in a holiday mood. As she waited for a space in the crowd so she could exit, Abby saw every table fill. Impulsively, she turned back toward Jenny.

"Want some help? I'm very experienced!"

Jenny grinned. "I'm in charge today, so you're hired."

This could be a small adventure to talk about later, Abby thought as she tied an apron around her waist and threw her purse behind the register.

"Get ready for the real Yellowstone," said Jenny. "Hungry tourists!"

Hungry tourists who kept Abby running for two hours straight, using muscles she'd forgotten she owned. But who also left her nice gratuities.

"It was a lot of fun for me," she said to Jenny as she returned the apron. "All my college experience paid off, in more ways than one." She patted the windfall in her pocket. "I'd forgotten about this little bonus."

"You did great. Want to earn more tonight?"

Abby paused. Why not? Waitressing was about as far from a therapist's practice as she could get. She nodded.

Late that night she fell asleep in her motel room

as soon as her weary body sank into the soft mattress beneath it. No dreams invaded her mind. No shadows lurked in the corners of her consciousness.

She woke to sunshine and peace. And a plan. I *need physical work. The harder, the better.* A guaranteed prescription for a good night's sleep. She reached for the phone.

"Good morning, Aunt Mo. It's your traveling niece... No, I'm not close yet...but I'm wondering if you know of any jobs available near you. I need a physical job. One that will knock me out at night. Something outdoors in the beautiful New England sunshine would be great."

"So, it's not a vacation from your troubles you're after? Like your mother told me?"

Her aunt's voice still lilted with a touch of Irish as she repeated Abby's mother's words. "My vacation is whatever works," Abby replied. "And I'm thinking that being idle won't do it. Besides, the pocket money would be a nice bonus!"

"Hmm," Maureen replied. "Let me think a moment. Let me... Ah, yes. Of course. My good friend, Elinor Templeton, and her sons own an apple orchard, and we're going into the harvest season right now. Timing's good."

"Apple picking?" Abby closed her eyes, imagining row after row of leafy green trees weighed down with ripe red fruit. A pretty picture. Seasonal work. No long-term responsibilities. And she'd certainly sleep well at night.

"That sounds perfect, Aunt Maureen. I'd appreciate consideration."

"Hmm," Maureen repeated slowly. "I guarantee that after I speak with Elinor, you'll get more than consideration. You'll have a job."

"I'll be there by Friday," replied Abby with enthusiasm. "Ready to pick apples."

JAKE TEMPLETON REACHED for the phone as he did every evening from his condo in Boston and dialed the farmhouse in Sturbridge. He glanced at his watch, making sure he wasn't extending Stacey's bedtime. He knew his daughter waited for his nightly call.

Of course, she hardly spoke once she was on the phone, and it was Jake who had to keep the conversation rolling. A conversation punctuated with "I love you's" from his end and a whispered acknowledgment from hers. It twisted his gut. But maybe if he kept hammering away at her, she'd truly believe him one day.

"Hi, Stace," he said in response to Stacey's greeting.

"I knew it was you, Daddy."

"That's my girl! Smart as always and with X-ray vision." In the old days his comment would have made her giggle. Not tonight. "How was your day?"

"Okay."

"What did you do?"

"Nothing much."

"How's Grandma?"

"Fine."

Now they were into the "pulling teeth" part of the conversation. "Can I talk to Betsy, please?" A desperate move.

"Oh, Daddy! Dogs don't talk on the phone!"

Was that a giggle? Coupled with the exasperation of a typical young daughter? He swore he'd go to clown school if that's what it took to get her to laugh.

"Betsy Ross does," he insisted. "Put her on." He could picture Stacey turning to her constant companion as he heard her faint voice across the wires.

"Betsy, he wants to talk to you."

"Woof."

"Hi, Betsy." He raised his voice. "How's my favorite hairy hound?"

"Ah—woooo," sang the canine in reply.

He almost dropped the phone. "And how's my daughter?"

"Woof. Woof." The two sharp barks brought Stacey back on the line.

"Daddy! You're driving her crazy. She's walking back and forth looking for you."

"One more day, baby. And I'll be home."

"Tomorrow's Friday," said Stacey.

"Right," he confirmed.

"And you're not on call?"

"Right again," he said.

"Good."

"I love you, Stace."

Silence.

His child loved him, too. He knew it. He felt it. But he didn't understand why she couldn't say it. Nothing would stop him from finding out the reasons, he vowed, although he knew he was taking a chance by digging in. A chance that he could lose her love altogether if the truth about her mom's accident ever came out.

A minute later, Jake blinked rapidly as his mother's voice came at him through the phone. He tried to focus on her words. Something about hiring Maureen Cooper's niece for the apple season. He shrugged. He'd known his mother's best friend and her deceased husband for years, and his mom was in charge of hiring. If Maureen's young niece needed a job, who was he to say otherwise?

"And she's going to live in the guest cottage because Maureen's efficiency is too small for an extended visit, and the women's bunkhouse is full."

Again he shrugged. "Is she taking a semester off from college to refinance herself?" he asked idly.

"She's thirty-one years old," laughed his mother.

"With a doctorate in psychology. I think schooldays are the farthest thing from her mind right now."

Jake felt himself stiffen when he heard the word *psychology*.

"A psychologist, Mom? Why is she really coming here?"

He heard the hardness in his voice, sensed his mother's hesitation. "Out with it, Mother. Did you import her for Stacey?"

He wouldn't put it past his mom. Had she and Maureen set this up? For God's sake, he knew they were both worried about Stacey. He was too! But didn't they see how hard he was trying to get through to his daughter?

"No, Jake! I'd never do that. Not without talking to you."

He relaxed a fraction and took a deep breath. "Okay, then," he continued mildly. "So what's her story?"

"She's a lovely girl, Jake," insisted Elinor Templeton.

He prayed for patience. "She may be, but why is she picking apples instead of practicing the profession she chose, the one that doesn't seem able to help many people?"

He heard the frustration in his own voice, frustration tinged with disappointment and a touch of contempt. Stacey had seen four different therapists in two years, and still she had not returned to anything close to the outgoing happy child of her younger days.

"Abby's coming here, son, because she needs a change of pace," replied Elinor to his question. "Everyone can benefit from a new environment once in a while. And although she'll be an orchard worker, she'll also be our guest, so I expect you to welcome her and behave yourself."

The last words surprised him. His mom hadn't used that tone with him since he was a teenager himself.

"Consider my hand slapped," he said. "But keep her away from Stacey. I don't need any more complications, especially from a shrink type who's gone into hiding."

ON FRIDAY AFTERNOON, Jake pulled into the long private road running alongside acres of apple trees and headed toward his family's spacious home at Templeton Orchards. The sedate farmhouse-style house had always been a happy place, very welcoming with its deep front porch running the entire width of the dwelling, providing plenty of room for rocking chairs, baby carriages and visitors. The week's responsibilities seemed to ease from his shoulders as he approached, and he breathed deeply, enjoying the mixed scent of ripening apples and freshly mown lawn.

Perhaps the weather also contributed to his high

spirits. Late afternoon toward the end of August provided a comfortable warmth without oppressive humidity. Nothing beat summer in New England. Jake appreciated every day of it perhaps because the season was so short here. In another week or so, he'd sniff autumn in the air. But more than the house, the weather and the beautiful countryside, Jake was eager to see his daughter.

He rounded the last curve and spotted Stacey— her dark wavy hair pulled back into a high ponytail—seated on the porch steps with faithful Betsy lying beside her. One thin arm was draped over the dog's neck while the other hand held a book in her lap. Jake smiled at the picture they made, glad that Stacey was as eager to see him as he was to see her.

He wondered what she was reading this week, or rather, this day. His daughter's appetite for books, both fiction and nonfiction, was enormous. From fantastical Harry Potter, to biographies of Helen Keller or Clara Barton, to articles devoted to apple harvesting, she read them all. Whatever might be interfering with her normal life and emotional well-being hadn't affected her love of reading. She had a curious mind and he was proud of that.

He drove to the side of the house, got out of the car and walked back to where his daughter waited.

"Hi, Stacey," he called, forcing himself not to rush at her, but opening his arms.

She put her book aside, stood up and started walking toward him. Slowly.

Come on, Stace. Step on it. I love you.

But she approached at her own deliberate pace, looked up at him, smiled and stepped into his arms, accepting the bear hug he gave her. A full thirty seconds passed until he felt her relax against him. And he knew that was about as much as he was going to get from her. The reserve she showed— even to him—was a trait developed since the accident. He didn't understand why she kept him at bay. Worse, he couldn't overcome it.

"Hey, Betsy," he acknowledged as the collie ran in circles around the two of them. She wagged and woofed with excitement and Jake sighed at the contrast between Betsy's joyful greeting and his daughter's subdued one.

"So how's my best girl?" he asked as he kissed the top of Stacey's head.

"Fine," she answered. "We've been busy today picking blueberries."

"Yum. Pies!"

She giggled and glanced up at him. "Grandma said you'd eat them all if we let you."

He swooped down to kiss her on the nose. "And she'd be right. Blueberries are my favorite."

"Ooh, Daddy. Don't let anyone hear you say that. We sell apples here."

Jake laughed with delight. "Nine years old," he

said with a grin, "and already thinking about the bottom line. Grandma and Uncle Robert have created a coldhearted businesswoman, no doubt about it. Now, where is that mother of mine?"

Stacey smiled and pulled his hand. "Come on. She's interviewing some people in the office. But she said to let her know when you arrived."

Jake rested his arm around his daughter and walked the two hundred feet down the road to the business office.

He heard the conversational voices of women before he opened the door. He recognized his mom's voice, of course, then picked up on Maureen Cooper's pleasant tone, and then a huskier voice, sexy, young...and he remembered Maureen's niece. Damn! He didn't need a wild card in the deck right now.

Grimacing, he pushed the door open and walked into the room. Then wished he'd taken more time. He felt Stacey stop at his side, her hand groping for his, and flicked his gaze downward where her little chest was rising and falling as she stared at the woman speaking with her grandma.

"Daddy," she said in a not-so-soft whisper, "I think...I mean Betsy thinks...that the lady over there...sort of...looks a lot like Mommy."

A wild card all right, dealt from the bottom of the deck.

CHAPTER THREE

THE THREE WOMEN were silent following Stacey's remark. Jake stared at the stranger, his initial shock at the resemblance to Claire tapering off the longer he studied her.

"Not really, Stace," he said in the most casual voice he could muster. "Her hair may be the same shade of reddish-brown and just as wavy, but this lady's eyes are as round as circles, not tilted. And her voice is different, too."

"Would you like my dress size?" asked the female in question as she rose from her chair.

She was a pretty woman, all right. Not too happy at the moment, if her expression was a barometer. Taller than Claire, a bit too slender for her frame, but she moved with physical energy and grace. It was that husky timbre in her voice, however, that set her apart. A Kathleen Turner voice. Or Lauren Bacall. Sexy. Different. He'd never confuse her with Claire. Thank God.

He walked toward Maureen's niece and extended his hand. "Sorry about that," he began. "I'm Jake

Templeton and this is my daughter, Stacey. Your dress size can remain a secret for as long as you like.''

A slow smile traveled across her face as she clasped his hand. Her dark brown eyes twinkled, and Jake revised his opinion. Not pretty. Beautiful. The kind of beauty that takes a person by surprise. The kind that makes a person want to see more smiles. Another person, maybe, but not Jake Templeton. He had a daughter to protect.

"Hello, Jake. And hello, Stacey. I'm Abby MacKenzie, your newest employee." Abby smiled at Stacey and shook her hand. "And who's this?" she asked as she scratched the collie behind the ears. The dog's tail slowly started waving back and forth, before picking up speed and creating a breeze with its featherlike fan.

"This is Betsy," replied Stacey eagerly. "Betsy Ross. She's my best friend."

Jake winced. He saw Abby's eyes narrow for an instant before she smoothed out her expression.

"Seems to me," she said to Stacey, "that Betsy's lucky to have *you* for a friend."

Stacey beamed at the compliment, and Jake watched her in amazement. It had taken less than two minutes for this stranger to win a spontaneous smile from his daughter.

He finally turned to his mother and her friend Maureen, both of whom had been quiet until now.

One look at their faces and he understood why. They were totally focused on Abby and him. Finally, his mom waved him over and he bent down to kiss her.

"Welcome home, son," Elinor greeted, her blue eyes sparkling. "The weekend doesn't come soon enough." She glanced at the older woman and Jake smiled at Maureen.

"Hi, Maureen," he said, giving her a peck on the cheek. And that's when he recognized the same gleam in her eye as he'd seen in his mom's. No doubt about it. The women were planning something.

He said nothing, however, knowing that with time any matchmaking plan would dissipate. Jake had no place in his life for romance, especially with a psychologist. His time was devoted to Stacey and his career.

"Abby's car is already at the guest cottage," said Elinor. "Do you think you could give her a hand with the luggage?"

"I don't need any help, Mrs. Templeton," said Abby before Jake could respond. "I've been managing perfectly well on my own for years. No need to change now."

"But evening's coming, and you don't know your way around yet. Your busy aunt—the star of the community's fall musical, *Hello, Dolly!*—doesn't even have time to stay for dinner, so she's no help." Elinor flashed Maureen a look of amused exasperation before returning a serious gaze to Abby. "I'm sure you'll want to unpack and settle in a bit before we eat."

Jake could see through his mother's guise. Suddenly the astute sixty-three-year-old woman who ran the orchard with a backbone of steel—the woman whose interview style could be mistaken for a police interrogation—was concerned about a perfectly healthy young woman taking a short walk to the cottage.

"I'll help Ms. MacKenzie, Grandma," said Stacey. "Betsy and I can show her around."

Jake looked at his daughter's eager face and knew he'd be unloading the trunk of a California vehicle in the next five minutes. There was no way on earth he'd allow Stacey to go off alone with a psychologist masquerading as an orchard worker. He'd keep reminding himself of that despite her warm brown eyes and sultry voice. Not to mention that killer smile.

WHY WAS HE LOOKING at her as though she might kidnap the child? Abby hadn't asked him for help. Didn't want his help. In fact, he'd made her uncomfortable from the moment he and Stacey had stepped into the office. Too bad about her resemblance to his dead wife. It might startle the kid, but Abby was sure Jake would have no trouble differentiating between the two women.

She shrugged. Let him think whatever he wanted. She wasn't planning any relationship with him, so she didn't have to think about him at all. Just be polite at dinnertime—she was a guest as well as an employee—and keep to herself. Her goal was to pick apples all day and sleep soundly at night. Period. No hidden agendas. She looked forward to Sunday when Elinor Templeton and her older son, Robert, would hold an orientation for all the seasonal helpers. She looked forward to a simple routine.

"Ready to go, Dr. MacKenzie?" asked Jake.

Surprised at the use of her title, she whirled toward him and stopped. No denying the challenge in his eyes, his stance. Body language spoke volumes in her line of work, and she could read his loud and clear. *Let's get this over with, Doctor of Psychology MacKenzie.* So he didn't like people messing with his mind. Now even Stacey seemed to have lost her enthusiasm as she hovered next to her dad. Didn't he know that kids picked up signals from trusted adults as quickly as the brain sent messages to the hand touching a hot stove?

Not her problem. "I'm as ready as you are, *Dr. Templeton,*" she replied, walking toward the door and waving to her aunt. "See you tomorrow afternoon, Aunt Mo. Knock 'em dead tonight."

Maureen laughed. "We don't knock 'em dead until opening night, my dear, and that's two months away. But thanks for your good thoughts and understanding. Tonight's actually the first rehearsal and the cast needs me there.''

Her aunt was terrific. Trim, active, a woman who never met a stranger. And now part of an amateur but skilled thespian group where her voice and talent would be appreciated. Abby turned back from the door and walked to Maureen. Gave her a hug. ''I'm so glad to see you,'' she whispered.

''Same here,'' came the reply. ''And maybe,'' the older woman whispered, ''while you're here, you can do some good.'' She glanced quickly at Jake and Stacey before squeezing Abby's hand. ''There's a lot of pain there.''

A snapshot of Officer Conroy lying on her office floor flashed through Abby's mind, and her heart jumped in her chest. ''Sorry, Aunt Mo, there's pain everywhere. I can't help.''

Abby walked to the exit where Jake, Stacey and the dog waited. ''I'm ready now. Even have the key to the cottage.''

Jake grunted as he opened the door and let her pass in front of him.

Abby sighed. It seemed like a long evening lay ahead. She shrugged and turned her attention to the landscape around her.

She saw beauty. Lush trees—tall, strong oaks—standing like sentinels with full-branched maples alongside in copses behind the asphalt road connecting the business office to the white clapboard main house. Abby tilted her head to scan the distance to the cottage and saw that the trees continued to that area too. In the farther distance, she saw apple trees. Row after row, they filled green fields as far as her eye could see.

"It's gorgeous," she breathed, and paused when Jake did, watched him survey the surroundings.

"Yes," he said. "It is. Sometimes I forget."

The sun hid behind rolling hills to the west, leaving cooler temperatures typical of the season, while the remaining rays cast long pale fingers across the ground. Abby sniffed experimentally. Grass, earth, hay, dew. Evening in the country, New England style. She liked it. Maybe this vacation would work out after all.

They walked forward almost in unison, Abby feeling completely relaxed for the first time that day. Relaxed and a bit tired. A good feeling.

As they approached her Mazda a moment later, Stacey's small voice interrupted Abby's thoughts. "What kind of doctor are you, Dr. MacKenzie? The stomachache, sore-throat kind or the just talking kind? Or maybe a cardiologist like Daddy?"

Abby heard a thread of hope in the last suggestion the child made, but didn't quite understand it. In fact, she didn't fully understand the entire question. The talking kind? Unless... Of course—a psychologist. How else would a child describe it?

"Right now, Stacey, I'm not practicing any doctoring at all. I'm on a three-month vacation. It's called a sabbatical."

"A sab-sabbatical?"

"That's right," said Jake. "A new word for your vocabulary list. It used to mean a paid year off given to college professors after seven working years so that they could travel or do research. But now, I guess it's used for anyone at anytime for anything."

He hadn't raised his voice; he hadn't glanced her way, but his definition was less than flattering. Abby felt her back straighten, her spine stiffen as she stood poised with her car keys in hand.

"Perhaps, Dr. Templeton, you might consider following my example. A little R&R—that's rest and...*reflection* to you—might cure a bad disposition."

Only the sound of chirping crickets invaded the silence that followed until, a moment later, those distinct songs were overpowered by Jake's laughter. Hearty, clean laughter at his own expense.

Abby watched, fascinated, as a transformation took place in front of her. The blue eyes, earlier laden with suspicion and distrust, now warmed, then simmered as his laughter filled the air. And the lean face, so intense from the moment he'd stepped into the office, was now relaxed, a smile lingering after the last chuckle left his throat. A handsome man by any standard, but so much more appealing now.

"My, my, my," said Abby. "What an improvement."

His eyebrow arched. His gaze captured hers and wouldn't release it. "Want to explain that?" he asked softly.

She stared into his probing eyes and shivered down to her toes. Fortunately, her antennae were as sharp as ever. She'd stick to her plan. No romance—just honest hard work.

She grabbed a tote bag from the trunk, opened the door to the cottage and waited for Jake to set her large suitcase inside.

"Daddy," called Stacey as she followed Jake into the guest quarters. "I want a sabbatical, too. Just like Dr. MacKenzie."

Jake tugged gently on his daughter's dark ponytail and bent down to kiss her on the forehead. "You've just had a sabbatical, sweetheart. It's called summer vacation."

"Oh, no," she replied, wrinkling her forehead, but not missing a beat. "*Everyone* gets that. But *I* want a sabbatical from the whole fourth grade. For the whole year."

Whoops! Abby watched Jake absorb his daughter's statement. Watched a reservoir of sorrow eclipse his normal expression for a moment, and knew her aunt was right. There was pain here. And there was love.

Abby had no intention of getting involved with either.

THIRTY MINUTES LATER, Abby threw a sweater over her shoulders, opened the cottage door and nearly fell over Jake as he raised his hand to knock.

"Steady there," he said, catching her by the elbow.

"Whoa! You startled me." His touch was warm; his hand secure on her arm. "I wasn't expecting an escort to walk a hundred and fifty feet. I can easily see the house from here." Her words raced into one another, and she felt breathless.

"True. But it's getting dark now, and you're not familiar with the grounds."

"Sounds like your mother talking," she laughed, stepping back and breaking their contact.

"I can't figure it," he admitted as they started walking to the big house. "My mom's not usually so protective. I know you're Maureen's niece, but did you get hurt recently? Break your ankle or a leg? Why is she so concerned?"

"Dr. Templeton," she said, keeping her voice steady, "I'm as healthy as the proverbial horse. Your mom has absolutely no reason to be concerned about anything."

Now she tilted her face to look at him, made eye contact and hoped she'd convinced him. Her business was *her* business. But Aunt Maureen had a lot to account for.

"Okay, then," he said as they approached the house. "Good." He paused before opening the door. "By the way," he added, "I owe you an apology for this afternoon. Please call me Jake. We're really not very formal around here."

For reasons she'd think about later, her spirits lifted. An apology from the guy who wished she'd never invaded his domain!

"Well, Jake, I accept your apology. Call me Abby. And Stacey can too, if that's all right with you."

He paused, then nodded thoughtfully. "I'll let her know."

"Good." She smiled at him, happy to be on a more comfortable footing with someone she'd be running into a lot. His eyes warmed, a grin started to cross his face. And suddenly he was looking at her the way a man looked at a woman he wanted to know better. Her heart raced into overtime. The man was lethal. Good-looking, smart, with a body that could warm a winter's night. She shivered.

"You're cold, Abby. Let's go in," Jake finally said, urging her forward. "The family's waiting."

Abby didn't think *waiting* was quite the right word. The family was there all right. Children and adults were everywhere. Two identical little blond boys raced their matchbox cars up and down the staircase leading to the second floor while Betsy stood in the middle of the stairs barking at them, watching them run past her and seemingly keeping an eye on all their activities.

Abby heard the soft drone of a television from the living room. She glanced in and saw a pregnant blond woman on the couch, her eyes closed, ignoring the TV, with her hands lying protectively on her stomach.

A big man with a strong resemblance to Jake came toward them, but his attention was on the children. "That's enough, boys. Outside until dinner. Now."

The boys scrambled, the dog with them.

"The noisemakers are my six-year-old twin nephews," explained Jake as they all watched the culprits race out the door. "They never get tired and they never stop."

"I can't argue with him," said Jake's look-alike.

Jake grinned and clapped the man on the shoulder. "No, you can't. They've been on the go since birth and they're all yours." He pulled Abby forward. "C'mon, say hello to my big brother, Robert."

"Hi, again," said Abby, extending her hand to Robert. She turned to Jake. "We met briefly this afternoon when your mom hired me."

"A lovely addition to the crew, I'd say," remarked Robert with a smile.

The two brothers could almost have been twins themselves, thought Abby. Robert's face was fuller, in fact, he was a little broader and heavier in general, but his sparkling blue eyes were the same as Jake's…and Stacey's…and Elinor's. In this family, blue dominated.

"Welcome to the orchard business and to our home." Robert shook her hand firmly. He turned to Jake, and his grin faded as he nodded toward the living room. "Susan's in there resting. This pregnancy is more difficult than the first one was. Ma chased her out of the kitchen." His creased forehead reflected the concern in his voice.

"You go keep her company, Rob," said Jake. "Abby and I will help out with dinner." He gently shoved his brother toward the living room and then led Abby to the busy country kitchen where the delicious aroma of roast chicken and sweet-potato pie made her stomach rumble.

"I didn't realize how hungry I was," she said as she entered the room.

"Well, there's plenty to go around," said Elinor emphatically from her position at the stove. "We cook big around here, Abby, and I want you to feel at home. The fridge is yours for as long as you stay." She tapped her soupspoon against the rim of the deep pot on the burner and gave Abby a quick head-to-toe once-over. "Maureen said you needed to put a few pounds back on and she was right."

Abby felt heat spread from her chest to the tips of her ears. She'd kill her aunt! Taking a deep breath, and for the second time that day, she said, "I'm as healthy as a horse, Elinor. Aunt Mo worries too much. Now, what can I do to help?" She pasted a smile on her face and tried to ignore Jake's gaze.

"I never turn down an extra pair of hands. So you can help Stacey set the table and Jake can toss this salad." Elinor pushed a large bowl of greens and fresh veggies toward her son.

Abby turned to face the child, who'd been quietly placing dinner plates around the pedestal oak table.

"Hello, Dr. MacKenzie." The subdued greeting was accompanied by a brief smile.

"Hi, Stacey," Abby replied. "You're welcome to call me Abby. Your dad says that we're very friendly around here."

Stacey's smile grew a fraction as she looked at her dad, a question on her face.

"'Abby' is fine, Pumpkin. It's hard to be formal when a person's climbing up and down apple trees. What if she gets a phone call? We'd have to run around the orchard with a megaphone calling, 'Dr. MacKenzie, Dr. Abby MacKenzie, call on line 2.'" Hands circling his mouth, his voice imitating a nasal operator found on any comedy channel, Jake paced the room as though searching for Abby.

"Oh, Dad-dy," came the exasperated reply. "You should be in Aunt Maureen's play." But a tiny giggle emerged, and the joy on Jake's face couldn't be missed.

Abby saw it all. The love this man had for his daughter was absolute. An image of her own dad came to mind as she'd kissed him goodbye before leaving on her journey East. She'd heard his gruff cop voice as he bear-hugged her.

"I still don't like this idea of yours. But you don't listen to anyone," he'd complained in exasperation. "So keep your doors locked. Don't pick up hitch-hikers. And tell your aunt to take care of you."

She'd embraced him hard, still so solid and strong, thankful for the love between them. Fathers and daughters. Special relationships.

Abby looked at the pair in front of her. They seemed as solid a pair as any, but…undercurrents rippled the surface. She'd already felt some of them. A child whose best friend was a dog? A child whose father visited only on weekends. A father who was desperate to make his child laugh.

Five minutes later, the table was set, the main course was being served family-style. A blueberry pie was warming in the oven. Abby sat next to Jake with Stacey on his other side. Elinor had directed the seating of the entire group, and Abby wondered if the woman was reporting back to Maureen the next day.

Robert's wife, Susan, had joined them at the table, but Robert didn't look too happy about it. Abby guessed that the petite woman had a whole lot of stubborn in her.

"Now how did you get the two imps in here so quickly with clean hands and faces?" Abby asked. The little boys now looked like a mother's dream, smelled of fresh soap, and were sitting quietly.

"Oh, that's easy," Robert replied. "Food. They'll do anything for food. Right, Sue?"

"They sure will. But it did take a little training, some tantrums and tears. I'd hate to go through that again."

"Too late, honey," joked Robert, pointedly looking at his wife's stomach. "But I hear that parents are much smarter the second time around."

"You and I will have to be," Sue retorted. "The kids will outnumber us!"

"At least there's only one this time," said Jake. "We couldn't survive another dose of double trouble." He winked at his nephews and grinned.

The boys giggled, totally adorable, and well pleased with themselves. Abby saw Jake glance at Stacey, his expression wistful. Easy to read him when his guard was down. If only his daughter could be as carefree as the boys...

General conversation began as the food was passed. Elinor asked Abby about the route she'd taken cross-country. "After Yellowstone," she said, "all I saw was highway. I knew I wanted to get to Aunt Mo's sooner rather than later."

Abby cast a glance at Jake, surprised to find him studying her as though she were a specimen under a microscope.

"Why the hurry?" he asked.

His question could have been idle curiosity, but Abby heard the suspicion in his voice. She held his gaze. "It's been too long since I've seen her."

A corner of his mouth turned upward, but the smile didn't travel farther. He obviously didn't trust her.

She could live with that. She wasn't out to impress him and she had no intention of joining the Templetons for meals on a regular basis. The guest cottage had a kitchen; she planned to use it. Suddenly Abby felt fatigue settling in. She smiled at the thought of a good night's sleep.

"A penny for them," said Jake.

She blushed. "Not worth even that much. Just thinking about uninterrupted sleep."

"You drove cross-country all alone in what? Three days? Four days? You should probably sleep for a week." His attention lingered. He pitched his voice so only she could hear him. "What was the real rush, Abby?" he asked again. "Running from something? Or someone?"

She felt the color drain from her face. The man was certainly astute. He had a keen eye, and she didn't like it. She could not spend three months under his scrutiny. Then she remembered he spent most of his time in Boston and relief filled her.

Feeling reckless, she pasted on her most brilliant smile and turned toward him. "I promise I'm not wanted by the police or the FBI, and I think, Jake, that's all you need to know. You said yourself that a sabbatical was often used for travel. So I traveled and landed here. End of story."

Jake's eyes darkened, and he shook his head. "I don't think so, Abby. Not the end of story. Not the end at all."

She couldn't think of an appropriate retort, but fortunately didn't have to. Stacey saved the day.

"Uncle Robert, I've got to tell you something." The child wasn't smiling. Abby wondered what was coming next.

"Uh-oh. I know that tone of voice," replied Robert. "It's something big. Did the boys mess up your bookshelves again?"

"Nope, not today. Anyway, you're going to have to meet the school bus every day this year because I'm going on a sabbatical like Abby. She skipped out on her job, and I'm skipping fourth grade and I'm very happy."

Abby winced. Seemed the new "vocabulary" word was making a lot of trouble. Of course, Abby had nothing to do with the girl and her desire to skip school. But she couldn't help wondering whether Jake would find some way of blaming her.

She glanced up to see him rolling his eyes at his daughter. "I thought we talked about this earlier, Stace. What is going on here tonight with you two ladies? I'm not buying into either of your stories."

"What's hard about buying in?" asked Robert. "Abby wants to pick apples and Stacey hates school. I hated school, too, until I got to college. Stacey is my niece through and through."

Jake groaned. "Keep encouraging her, Rob, and I'll tell her not to help you during the busy season...which I don't have to remind you is upon us."

"Yikes! We couldn't survive without Stacey. So, kiddo," Robert said, addressing his niece, "you'll just have to go to school. We need you."

Abby almost laughed at Stacey's expression.

"I don't see why I have to go," said the girl. "I want to be like Grandma. She never went to college and she runs the whole orchard. I want to run the whole orchard, too."

"But life was different when I was your age, sweetheart," said Elinor. "I didn't have the opportunity."

"And it didn't matter," Stacey retorted. "It won't matter for me, either."

Whoa! The conversation was getting hot. Abby looked around the table. Lots of people with lots of opinions but none making an impact on the kid. The child needed to *want* to go to school. Should Abby get involved in this family discussion? It was hard not to when her "talking doctor" instincts told her she could put Stacey on track. Abby leaned forward in her chair.

"It seems to me, Stacey, that running a successful orchard business these days requires not only ownership but leadership. They aren't the same things." Now Abby leaned across Jake to look at Stacey. "Templeton apples are special, right? They're the best."

Stacey nodded.

"And you'll always want them to be the best, won't you?"

The girl nodded again.

"How will you make sure of that without keeping on top of the industry? Without learning about soil quality and pest control? Just like your dad does research in cardiology and helps people stay well, other scientists are doing research to improve crops. You need to understand what they're doing so you can make sure Templeton Orchards will always be the best. It's a huge responsibility and much more scientific than when Grandma started the business. I bet that your Uncle Robert knows hundreds of things about running the orchard that you haven't thought about yet."

"Yes, but…I can already figure out how many bushels of apples we can get from one tree. Ever since I moved here, I learned as much as I could."

The kid was bright. No question. "Well, that's a start," Abby replied.

Stacey's face fell. "You mean I have to go to college and learn everything?"

"Only if you want to make good decisions. Only if you want to keep producing the best apples in Massachusetts or in the world! Only if you want to be a leader and have the respect of all the apple growers in New England." Abby leaned closer and pitched her voice lower. "The other choice, of course, is to just be a regular worker and let the twins run the company."

As she'd hoped, Stacey rose to the bait. "No way. I'm older and they're mostly pains in the neck. And they'd better do everything *I* say."

Now *that* statement sounded like the normal bossiness of an older sister. Abby glanced around the table. Everyone seemed to be choking on their laughter. Certainly Robert and Susan. Elinor, too. Abby looked up at Jake to see a quick smile, before he turned back to his daughter.

"So, what are you thinking now, Stace, or should I be afraid to ask?"

"Okay, okay," she grumbled. "I'll go to fourth grade. Who cares about all those stupid kids anyway?"

Bingo! The first clue dropped, and Abby's eyes met Jake's alert ones. *Take it from here, Jake. She's your daughter.*

"Let's take Betsy for a walk after supper, Stace. Just you and me and the hound."

"Sure. We can stay out late, way past bedtime."

Abby yawned spontaneously, but right on cue. "And I can't wait for my bedtime."

"We'll walk you to the cottage first," said Jake, "as soon as we clean up in here."

Could that be genuine gratitude in his voice? Abby smiled to herself. The poor guy really didn't know how to take her. Well, she certainly wouldn't lose sleep over his dilemma.

But an hour later, she wasn't so sure. Her body was limp under the covers, but her brain refused to shut down. Damn! She needed to sleep.

But the images of everyone she'd met that day superimposed themselves in her mind. Elinor Templeton, trim figure with stylish salt-and-pepper hair and a pencil behind her ear; Robert Templeton, with his competent, steady presence; Susan, a petite, pregnant and strong-willed match for her husband; two adorable and identical little boys; a beautiful long-haired collie devoted to her mistress; Stacey Templeton, a pretty and intelligent girl accustomed to hiding her feelings.

But the image that returned most often was of a high-energy six-footer, with a strong, lean masculine face dominated by a pair of blue eyes. Observant blue eyes. Suspicious blue eyes. Warm…cold…hot… No, they hadn't been hot. But she could picture them full of heat…and passion.

She laughed at herself and punched her pillow. He wasn't her type at all. But maybe there was a message here, a message about her nonexistent social life. When she returned to California, she vowed, she'd make more time for personal interests. Maybe this journey was as much about self-discovery as about recovering from Officer Conroy's tragic death.

She took a deep breath and felt herself relax. Yes, she'd remedy her deficient personal life as soon as she returned to the West Coast. In the meantime, she'd stick to picking apples.

CHAPTER FOUR

AT TEN-THIRTY the next morning, Abby unloaded two bags of groceries from her car. The staples would supplement the communal meals she'd take with the other workers. Templeton Orchards treated their seasonal staff well, most of whom came from Jamaica and Mexico, with the balance from the local area. A cook and a helper had been hired to provide lunch sacks and hot dinners for everyone. They also made sure a breakfast buffet with urns of hot coffee was available every morning.

She'd learned a lot from listening to the Templeton family talk about the business last night, and looked forward to the more formal orientation the next day. Apples were one of her favorite fruits, but except for tales of Johnny Appleseed, she'd never thought much about them. She suspected she'd learn a great deal this season.

Bright sunshine and azure skies lured her outside as soon as she'd stored her groceries in the kitchen of the charming cottage. And it was charming, thought Abby as she swept a glance over it. The entire decor was comfortable Colonial with highly polished hardwood floors sporting oval area rugs. Bright Indian-print blankets added color throughout the house. Smaller afghan throws adorned the skirted couch and chairs, creating an inviting, cozy atmosphere, and a small brick fireplace—already stacked with wood—enhanced the homey feeling. Cozy. Homey. Charming. She could be happy here for three months.

She grabbed her sunglasses, stuck her keys in the pocket of her jeans and closed the cottage door behind her. It was a perfect day to explore her new surroundings. She took the two steps down from the small covered porch and then crossed the ten-foot front lawn to the hard-packed gravel road. The road ran from the cottage to the main house, before one branch cut a swath through acres of apple trees, while the other connected them to the county road. If she stuck to the orchard road, she couldn't get lost.

As she neared the farmhouse, she heard children's laughter floating on the air. It was a nice sound. She glanced toward them and saw Stacey throw a Frisbee to her young cousins, but the big collie caught it instead.

"No fair, no fair," the boys shrieked, trying to wrest control of the toy from Betsy.

Abby laughed at the predicament and waved. Instantly she was surrounded by three children and a dog.

"Where ya' goin', Abby?"

"Whatcha doin'? Can you play?"

Two identical toothless grins beseeched her, but it was the more serious older child who asked, "Would you like us to take you around the orchard, Abby? Then you won't get lost."

Abby looked at the three young faces. Who would be in charge of whom? "Stacey, why don't we ask your aunt or grandma if it's okay to leave the yard?" She'd follow Susan's or Elinor's lead.

"Aunt Sue is resting but Grandma's in the office."

Elinor seemed delighted with the plan. "Susan's got to stay off her feet as much as possible. This baby is too anxious to see the world. And I'm trying to stay on top of all the paperwork. Tomorrow is a big day." She then bent down and looked her grandsons in the eyes. "I'm counting on you boys to teach Abby about the apples and make sure she doesn't get lost. Deal?" She extended her hand.

"Deal, Grandma," said one.

Abby thought his name was Jonathan and his brother's name was Mac. But it might have been the other way around.

"Deal, Grandma," said the second boy. "We won't lose her, will we, Stacey?"

"No, we won't," replied Stacey. "And we won't

lose you either. Maybe we can catch up with Daddy and Uncle Robert. They've been out for hours. I think they went to the Preservation Orchard.''

Elinor looked at Abby with the Templeton twinkle in her eye. ''I hope you enjoy your tour, and by the way, don't worry about the kids. Keeping track of them won't be as difficult as you might think. You'll see why for yourself.''

In the beginning, Abby felt like the Pied Piper as the foursome marched down the road. A rather nervous Pied Piper. Being surrounded by children was unusual for her, and she also felt responsible, constantly checking that both boys were still with her and not wandering through the trees.

After about ten minutes, however, she realized she had nothing to worry about. Betsy was doing the work. The dog was herding all of them, including her! Each time Jonathan or Mac wandered into the rows of trees to play tag or get a ''perfect'' apple, Betsy barked softly, circled behind them, and with her head, nudged the child back to the path. The dog constantly trotted in front and in back of them doing her job.

Abby laughed to herself. Obviously Elinor had known that Betsy would do her thing. Abby wondered for a moment if Jake would find this discovery as funny as she did, and then dismissed the thought. Jake probably knew all about Betsy's instincts. Probably bought the dog because of them. All part of his protective instincts where Stacey was concerned.

"Would you like me to explain about the orchards, Abby, or would you just rather walk?" Stacey sounded so grown-up. Her adult tone of voice, the options presented in the question itself, and her patient demeanor sounded more like an adult than a nine-year-old.

Abby studied her carefully. "Last night you told me that you knew a lot about the orchards. Was that true?"

"Oh, yes!" No mistaking the eagerness she showed.

"Okay, then. I like to learn new things everywhere I go. Shoot."

"We've got two hundred acres and grow different kinds of popular apples, like Macintosh and Jonathan—and that's how Mac and Jon got their names—and Delicious, Golden Delicious, Courtland, Granny Smith, Rome Beauty, Winesap…and, I forget sometimes…oh, yeah, Baldwin and Empire. And we also have a special Preservation Orchard where Daddy and Uncle Robert are working with Old Sturbridge Village to bring back some of the old-fashioned apples."

Abby had known about Old Sturbridge Village from girlhood trips to visit her aunt. OSV was a re-created rural community from the 1830s with a working farm, costumed interpreters and hands-on demonstrations of the way things used to be done.

Abby listened as Stacey continued to describe the characteristics of trees, some of the problems they had with pests and marketing. She sounded as knowledgeable as a graduate from agricultural school. She certainly was an intelligent young woman. Too bad she didn't know how to be a child.

"Tell her about the fun stuff," said one twin.

"Yeah. We got a little zoo with lambs and chickens," added his brother.

"And we got a hay wagon and we give rides."

"And we make apple cider right in the cider house and everybody can watch. And we make candy apples and caramel apples."

"We sell 'em."

"Yeah. Millions and millions of people come to see us and they buy all our good stuff."

"I should hope so, silly. That's how we make our living." Stacey looked at Abby and rolled her eyes.

Abby tried to hide her grin as she watched the girl keep the little boys in line.

"It sounds as if we're going to be very busy next week getting all these apples and goodies ready for everyone," Abby said. "I bet your dad wishes he was home more often during this busy time."

Stacey's instant grin lit up her face. "But he will be, Abby. Daddy always takes a two-week vacation during the season.'' She looked dreamy for a moment. "And that's the best part...."

Two straight weeks! The information caught Abby off guard. But she wouldn't run into him much, she reassured herself. She wasn't on his list of favorite people, far from it. They'd definitely stay out of each other's way.

She and the children had been keeping a steady pace through the orchard as they talked. Now Abby glanced left and right trying to get her bearings, realizing that the original road had long since ended. She turned in a full circle and saw lush trees with fruit-laden branches everywhere. Everything looked the same; there were no landmarks. It was embarrassing to think that she'd need Betsy to lead her back to the cottage.

"Stacey, do you ever get lost in here?"

"Not anymore. When I was little I did though. After my mom...my mom died and I came to live here. I remember when Daddy found me. He squeezed me so hard, I couldn't breathe. I got scared and started crying because he was crying, and Daddy *never* cries. And the very next day, we got Betsy. With Betsy around, Daddy said that he wouldn't have to worry."

Abby could easily imagine Jake taking quick action to prevent Stacey from wandering off again. She'd have been only seven years old at the time. A scary incident.

"And you don't have to worry about getting lost, either," continued Stacey. "See, the trees are planted in wide rows. And if you stay between two rows, sooner or later you'll come out on the road that goes home. But if you're afraid, I'll take you anywhere you want to go if it's okay with Daddy."

"I think the only place I'll be going is *up* a tree."

Betsy's excited barking drew Abby's attention. Jake and Robert were approaching and the dog was in a frenzy racing between her two groups of favorite people. Mac and Jon immediately made a running leap onto their father, who just managed to retain his balance.

"Hi, Stace. Looks like Betsy brought the family," said Jake as he hugged his daughter and petted the dog with approval. Then he turned to Abby.

"Good morning, Abby," he said.

"Good morning." He looked as good today as he had last night, maybe better, in worn jeans that hugged his long legs and a short-sleeve jersey that outlined solid lean muscle.

"Sleep well in your new quarters?"

"Absolutely," she replied. "It's a lovely little house."

He nodded. "I hope you'll enjoy it while you're with us."

In other words, don't overstay the welcome. "I'm sure I will." It was time to change the subject. "The orchards are beautiful, very impressive, and your daughter's knowledge about them even more so.''

His eyes strayed to Stacey and focused there. ''She's a smart one, all right.'' He sighed, but then smiled. ''And from the sound of her conversation last night, she's got her career all picked out at the ripe old age of nine. The women in my family are strong-minded from the get-go.''

Abby grinned. She liked a man who appreciated strong women. ''But she *is* only nine, Jake. She could change her mind a thousand times between now and whenever.''

A chuckle escaped him. ''Maybe. But my mother never did. She's as much married to the land as my father was.''

And Stacey spent more of her time with her grandmother than with Jake.

''But you're her dad, Jake. In the end, she could choose medicine,'' said Abby, reacting to the unspoken thought. ''Obviously, the farming life didn't hold you.''

''Hell, I don't care what she chooses as long as she's happy.'' He paused. ''Now, there's an elusive word in my daughter's life.'' He turned toward his brother. ''Take the kids back for lunch, will you? I'm giving Abby a personal tour.''

''A most excellent idea, Jake,'' replied Rob as he motioned to the kids. ''Let's go, troops!''

And suddenly all was quiet in the orchard. A

slight breeze ruffled the leaves above Abby's head. She turned to Jake. "The orchard's beautiful, but I don't need a personal tour. I imagine I'll become well acquainted with the land and the apples in the days ahead."

He nodded. "That's a fact, so I won't mince words, Abby. The truth is, I wanted time alone with you, and we shouldn't be interrupted here."

What was coming now? He obviously had something on his mind and was doing a good job keeping a poker face. However, she was good at hiding her thoughts, too. Occupational training, she supposed.

"You've made a big impression on Stacey," Jake began without preamble, "and I'm worried." He stopped short and pivoted to look right at her. "I don't know anything about you, and that concerns me. Yes, you're Maureen Cooper's niece, and that would be enough for me if Stacey weren't so vulnerable."

Abby felt herself bristle. "What do you think I'm going to do to her?"

"Why do you need a three-month hiatus from the career you chose?" he asked, ignoring her question. "It's unusual that a young professional like yourself finds the need for a 'sabbatical.' It could be that you deserve all the sympathy in the world and need time off. On the other hand, you might be a lousy therapist, like so many I've encountered. I have a daughter to protect, Abby, and need to know the truth. So, tell me, what's your story?''

HE KNEW he'd stepped over the line when her eyes blazed lightning bolts at him. How could big, warm, chocolate-brown eyes change into points of fire? Suddenly his own blood felt as hot as Abby's eyes looked. A scorching heat racing through him from head to toe.

What irony! Could he be attracted to a woman he'd have to steer clear of? For Stacey's sake.

"All you need to know, Dr. Templeton," said Abby, "is that I'm here to work in the orchards. Yes, I needed a change of pace, but I am in no way a danger to your daughter or to you."

She sounded in control. But the corners of her mouth trembled, and Jake saw the vulnerability hiding there. Remorse caused him to back off.

"Nothing is more important to me than my daughter, Abby. I'm sure you can understand that. She used to be full of joy. Totally uninhibited and happy. It's been two years since her mother's death, but she hasn't adjusted at all. Stacey is hurting inside and I can't reach her. God knows I've tried. And the members of your profession—all four of them— have not helped either.''

His breathing came hard; the normal rhythm was broken. He knew he might be insulting Abby right now, but he took a cleansing breath and jumped in.

"I would appreciate it, Abby, if you don't get involved with her. We haven't had any luck with the shrink types, and I don't know anything about your professional credentials."

Her complexion paled, and he knew he'd been right when he'd suggested she was running from something. Something big and something bad. But thank God he'd discovered it. He didn't need Stacey suffering from any fallout.

"You're right, Jake. You don't know me and you love your daughter." Her husky voice was a bit lower than usual, but steady. She tilted her head back to meet his gaze. "So I'll relieve your mind completely. By the time you sit down to dinner tonight, I'll be gone. There are other orchards needing workers." Her eyes flashed at him now, not in anger but in challenge. *Will that make you happy?*

No way! "You're an intriguing woman, Dr. MacKenzie. And a compassionate one. And I hope you don't choose to find a job somewhere else." Relief came to him just by saying the words. A clarification of his feelings. Then he felt himself smile. "How would I ever explain your departure to Maureen and my mother?"

Someone else might have retorted with anger, but Abby's lips started to quiver with a smile too, and she rolled her eyes.

"I'd like to be a fly on the wall when you try to explain my absence to them."

But he wasn't finished. "I still have to protect Stacey. You'll leave by Thanksgiving, and I know Stacey can't handle another goodbye to someone she's grown fond of."

"I have no intention of getting involved with anyone here," said Abby, her chin thrust forward, "child or adult."

His eyes widened. So did his mind. Who was she kidding? Abby was obviously a social being, the kind who couldn't help getting involved with others, as she'd proved with Stacey last night. Her behavior was loud and clear, and played counterpoint to her vocal protestations. Maybe the shrink needed to get better acquainted with herself.

ABBY STARED at Jake, all nerve endings on alert. He liked throwing down challenges, and she'd never been a coward about picking them up.

Jake seemed to be a shortsighted jerk about her profession; not every therapist matched well with every patient. But he'd mentioned four child psychologists. Seemed a fair number to have failed. On the other hand, Stacey had the intelligence to sabotage the entire venture if she wanted to by either miscommunicating or not communicating at all.

Although working with children had not been her ultimate goal, Abby had completed courses in child psychology as part of her required curriculum. She had little doubt that Jake's concern for his daughter was well founded. His child's personality had totally changed since her mother's death. He loved his daughter; his frustration was genuine, and she could imagine him researching to find the right psychologist to help Stacey.

But he hadn't succeeded.

No wonder her presence at his home unnerved him. And now she could tell she was unnerving him again as she stared into his eyes.

Her breath caught as his eyes darkened. Her fingertips tingled. Who was unnerving whom?

She broke contact first, turned away from him and started walking. She felt more than saw him stay by her side. The natural quiet surrounding them was broken only by a lone bumblebee flying slowly across their path before picking up speed and disappearing.

"I read somewhere," said Abby, "that apple growers lease hives of bees in the spring during blossom time to insure good pollination."

"That's true," said Jake.

She slowly turned her head from side to side, studying the trees. Her gaze fastened on a particularly tempting Macintosh apple hanging within reach just above her head. She raised both arms to pluck it, admiring how the red and yellow fruit sparkled in the sun.

Bright red on yellow. Red on yellow. A familiar pattern. She stared, transfixed...couldn't look away, couldn't move a muscle. She watched the apple morph into two, then slowly divide again into a dozen small clusters of red fruit, each cluster first floating, then flying, then reaching warp speed until crash-landing—*splat!* Large red splats against a pale yellow wall. *Her* wall, in *her* office. And suddenly she was there again. Standing in her office door-way…looking.…

She couldn't breathe. "No, no, no," she whispered, afraid to move, afraid to gaze down. She knew who she'd see; this time she was expecting it. Tom Conroy was her patient, her responsibility. She had to take care of him. But there was so much blood. Oh, God. Blood was everywhere.

"Oh, no! Oh, no! Ohmygod." A familiar litany, but she could think of no other words to deal with the horror before her. "Officer down! Officer down!" she sobbed. "I have to call… Send the police. Now! There's gallons of blood. Please somebody…help him…help. Ohmygod, he's dead. He's dead! I've lost him. He's my patient and…I've…lost…him.…"

From a far distance, she heard her name being called over and over again, like an insistent buzzing that wouldn't stop. She slapped it away.

"Come on, Abby. Hit me again and wake yourself up. Come back to me. Focus on me. Jake."

Jake. Why was he annoying her? He didn't even

like her. She felt so tired, she could barely move her arms. What was going on?

Abby blinked, her eyelids opening and closing slowly several times. Finally she focused on Jake sitting on the ground next to her.

"Welcome back, Abby," he said quietly. "Take your time and tell me where you are."

She scanned the orchard, feeling Jake's fingers on her wrist, seeing him check his watch. "You're taking my pulse," she announced as though observing a lab experiment.

"Yeah. You're right. Why am I doing that?"

Her heart raced. She shivered as nightmare fragments floated in and out of her memory.

"Damn! I had another flashback." Abby jumped to her feet fully awake. She twirled away from Jake and strode down the aisle between the trees. "Damn, damn, damn!"

The memories had chased her for three thousand miles. She thought she'd break free of them through physical exhaustion and a complete change of routine. But obviously it wasn't going to be that easy. Well, she'd definitely call Martin today, regardless of their schedule. And she'd start keeping a journal to follow her own progress. She could certainly do for herself what she'd always done for her patients, she decided as she recalled the meticulous notes she kept in each patient file.

Her mind now set on a course of action, she

turned once more to Jake. "I'll be okay. I know what I have to do."

She saw his eyes narrow as he studied her.

"You do?" he asked.

"Yes."

"So do I. Come here." He held out his hand.

Abby examined his concerned face, then fixed her gaze back to his outstretched hand. The hand of a friend? Or an M.D.? She studied him again. He wasn't laughing, hadn't even cracked a grin. Wasn't upset either, or annoyed. He was just…solid. His arm hadn't wavered an inch as he waited for her to connect, but the distance to his strong palm could have been measured in light-years. She knew it was her move. Did she really want to connect? She raised her eyes to him again and saw…understanding, patience, warmth.

She stepped closer and slowly placed her hand in his. His fingers tightened around hers, but he didn't say a word. She felt the quiet strength of his touch. A calming silence and renewed peace flowed through her.

"Abby," said Jake, "would you like to tell me more about what happened in L.A.?" He pressed her fingers. "Maybe if I understood…" His words trailed off, but Abby quickly filled in the rest.

"If you understood, then what? You'd be less suspicious of me?" She heard the frustration—the tinge of anger—in her voice.

"Let's just say," Jake replied softly, "I'd have more confidence and maybe I could be a friend. Maybe I could help."

She turned her head and studied him as they walked. She could have used a friend back home. Someone from the medical community, someone who might have understood what had happened to her patient without pity or condemnation of her. But only her family had gathered round her, strong and loving, and Martin Bernstein, who was always supportive of the staff. Her colleagues had sympathized but kept their distance; and the police force...well, she didn't want to think about their opinions of "shrink-types."

Jake seemed sympathetic now, ready to be open and listen. But spilling her guts to him would be a true leap of faith. After all, despite his smarts, concern and medical background, she barely knew him.

"Thanks for your offer," she whispered. "I know you mean well, but I've got it under control. And if I don't, you'll be the first to know. That's a promise."

He nodded and squeezed her hand again. "I'll hold you to it."

His touch held strength and comfort. Abby's breath caught, and suddenly she wanted to tell him. She needed to confide. More than that, she wanted his respect. She wanted his trust. People had never been afraid to allow Abby around their children.

"Jake?" she said.

He turned to her, a question in his eyes. She met his gaze and took a deep breath. "One of my patients died...no, not just died," she amended. "He shot himself in my office almost three weeks ago." She glanced away and took a deep breath before continuing. "It was about as bad as it could be, and I guess I'm not handling it very well." She peered up at him once more. "So now you know the big secret behind my spur-of-the-moment sabbatical."

CHAPTER FIVE

ABBY KEPT HER EYES glued to Jake's face. Would he consider her crazy? Probably.

"So you think you're the only physician who's ever lost a patient?" he asked.

"I'm not a medical doctor," she replied automatically. "I have a doctorate in psychology."

"Technicality," he said, brushing her objection aside. "You treat patients who come to you for help. So do I. And I can tell you it's never a walk-in-the-park when you lose one. Even if you expect it."

She remained silent for a moment. "But I never expect it."

"What?" he replied, his expression stunned.

"No, wait." Abby held her hand up for emphasis. "Of course I know about clinical depression. Sometimes I've had to protect patients from themselves by getting them on meds or meeting with them every single day until a small light beckons at the end of the tunnel. But this situation..." She shook her head. "This situation was different...*is* different from the ones *you* experience."

"Not so," said Jake. "Bottom line is that you lost a patient."

"You don't understand," Abby argued, her hands fisted at her sides. "He killed himself in my office! He knew I'd find him. How's that for a message?"

"Hmm, let's think about it," Jake replied quietly. "Have you ever considered that your patient might have felt safe in your office? That through all his emotional pain, you provided a haven. He even trusted you to fix everything afterward."

"But that's just it!" Abby's protest echoed her frustration. "I couldn't fix anything, let alone everything. *I couldn't fix him.*"

Jake halted, placed his hands on her shoulders and turned her around. He gently lifted her chin with his finger. "Listen to me, Abby. Listen hard. They don't teach you this in medical school, and certainly not in grad school. When you lose a patient, you grieve. It's normal. And it's normal to feel guilty while you're wondering if you missed something, if you paid enough attention to that patient. Were you too immersed in other pressures?

"Occasionally a patient of mine dies even when everything is technically right and I've been on top of the case. I recheck the files, I recheck my notes, the patient's history. And I know I haven't missed anything and death happened anyway."

She'd done all that, too. But there was still one

big difference. "*Your* patients don't *choose* to die," she whispered. "Seems that mine do."

"I don't imagine for a minute, Abby, that your patients—the cops—*choose* to be involved in such horrific situations that it's impossible for them to return to whatever 'normal' is."

His words made sense. "You mean, wrong time, wrong place?"

He nodded and pulled her closer, his forehead just touching hers. "All patients want a miracle and they think we can pull one out of a hat. They don't realize that we're just as human as they are—with a little more education."

Abby listened, aware of the reassurance of his touch. "But that's what they're seeking and paying for, aren't they? Competent care," said Abby.

"No," he said softly. "They want miracles."

JAKE WANTED to kiss her. For comfort, for encouragement, and for being a woman he could admire. Her description of the trauma that had instigated her trip to the East Coast revealed a woman who cared deeply, maybe too deeply, about her patients and her work. She was vulnerable now. On a rocky road to regaining her confidence both professionally and personally. He had no idea how many more times she'd revisit the scene of the tragedy in dreams, or rather, nightmares. But he had a feeling the flashbacks wouldn't end yet. And next time, she might very well be alone when it happened. Cripes! He couldn't look after her, too. He had a daughter to worry about.

Stacey was as vulnerable as Abby. And she came first.

He straightened and took Abby's hand. "I have a suggestion," he said, trying for a lighter tone.

She cocked her head.

"Stick to Granny Smith apples. Solid green with occasional white flecks. No red and no yellow."

Her warm smile, her glistening brown eyes and the pressure of her fingers in his palm almost made him rethink what he had to say next. But the thought of his daughter's sadness prevented him from changing his mind. He'd try to be gentle.

"Abby," he began, "when you first arrived, I was upset. I thought you'd been hired behind my back to use your skills on Stacey and me. Now I realize that's not the case.

"Under ordinary circumstances, I might consider you a blessing in disguise. But the truth is, you're not in great shape. Stacey's not in great shape. So I'm asking you not to encourage Stacey's friendship. Especially since you'll be gone in ninety days, and she'll feel deserted again." Any thoughts he might have had about a relationship with Abby were out of the question now. He'd be a concerned acquaintance to her. Period.

Her hand left his. He saw her square her shoulders and straighten her spine.

"Believe me, I'm not being critical," he added. "In fact, you could both use those miracles we talked about earlier. It'll take nothing short of that to get my real daughter back."

She stared at him, her lips pressed together. "Miracles are for fairy tales. It's hard work that goes into regaining stability, regaining a sense of happiness."

She was right, and he nodded. He'd be willing to bet anything that she knew her stuff. Well, almost anything. He wasn't willing to bet Stacey.

He watched her turn away from him, then pause before looking back. For the first time, she seemed indecisive.

"What did you mean about getting your 'real' daughter back?" Abby finally asked.

A kaleidoscope of memories flashed through his mind, all of an energetic little girl. Running, giggling and dancing in her pink tights and soft slippers. Oh, could that child dance! Even at six and seven, she'd been as graceful as a swan, as joyful and light as a butterfly. She *heard* the music and she *was* the music. Once upon a time.

He swallowed. "As you can imagine the accident changed her beyond…beyond belief. I just want to put some joy back in her life." That's all he could bring himself to say. No details. Nothing about Stacey being locked in the car and crying for hours waiting for help. Abby didn't need to know anything else. She wasn't going to be part of Stacey's world. Stacey wasn't her case.

As if she could read his thoughts, Abby said, "I'm on vacation, Jake. And you're right. I'm in no condition to help anyone. I'm barely able to help myself, at least for now."

Although he was relieved, her wan smile almost broke his heart.

"Your daughter's safe," she reiterated, her voice huskier than usual. "I won't go near her."

He nodded and walked her back toward the house.

HER AUNT MO KNEW everyone in Sturbridge. At least that's how it seemed to Abby after she drove into town later that afternoon to have dinner with Maureen. Ever-energetic, and excited about her new condo, her aunt insisted on showing off the landscaped grounds and introducing her niece to everyone she met along the way.

Her apartment was part of a two-story cluster, nestled among evergreens brightened by flowering shrubs and massive floral plantings. It seemed strange to Abby that Maureen, who'd owned her own home with her husband, Frank, and who'd spent so many hours nurturing her own garden, had chosen to make such a drastic change.

"What's the use of a big house at this point? With

Frank gone, and no children, I'd be alone too much."

"Alone?" Abby laughed. "Aunt Mo, your phone doesn't stop ringing. You could host a card party, a line-dance party and a bingo party and never have the same guests twice."

"And I love it." Maureen's eyes twinkled as she chuckled along with Abby. "I want to spend my time with my friends, doing things together, having fun, and also making a difference in the community. Soon I'll be helping Elinor and her troops on the weekends and earn a little money besides."

"Not picking apples and climbing trees!" Abby said, horrified at the image.

"Not picking," Maureen laughed. "Selling. I sell half-bushel shopping bags that the customers take into the orchards with them to fill up. They can pick whatever kind of apple they want and go directly to their vehicles afterward."

"That's all right, then."

"Of course, dear. Elinor and her sons have a huge pick-your-own operation. I've helped out for years. It's fun." Maureen's eyes shone with merriment, and Abby had to laugh with her.

"So I'll see more of you," Abby said. "How nice."

"Ach. I should have bought a two-bedroom unit," said Maureen. "Then there'd be plenty of room for a long visit."

"Oh, Aunt Mo! Don't even think it. A large apartment would probably have been twice the price. I'm fine at the cottage."

Her aunt's look held much speculation. "I'm glad to hear that. So, tell me about your morning. Have you crossed paths with Jake or Stacey?"

Maureen had the subtlety of a bull. There was no doubt in Abby's mind that Maureen and Elinor hoped Abby and Jake would be attracted to each other. Maureen might be a much-loved thespian in community theater, but she wasn't a good enough actress to fool her niece.

Abby took Maureen's hands in her own to get her attention. "I'm here to pick apples, Aunt Mo. I've got no interest in getting involved with either father or daughter. And they have no interest in me. So get the idea out of your mind. Okay?" She waited until she saw Maureen's reluctant nod.

"Thanks, Aunt."

"What a waste, what a waste," sighed Maureen. "They're such fine people. Such good people. That accident was a terrible thing. Claire was a lovely girl, from the South, you see. Had no business being behind the wheel in all that snow. Leaving that poor child to grieve. And Jake, too. They could sure use some of your help."

With a rueful laugh, Abby replied. "Trust me, Aunt. They'd be better off with almost anyone else."

But Maureen kept shaking her head and mumbling something about stubbornness from Abby's father's side of the family. She could not possibly have inherited that trait from her mother, Maureen's sister.

Abby sighed, but said nothing. There was no reason for Maureen to know about the flashback or Jake's request regarding Stacey. And there was certainly no need for Elinor to know. Jake and Abby were adults. They'd handle their own lives.

AT NOON on Sunday, Abby, along with about thirty others, was trying to absorb everything she needed to know about apple harvesting at Templeton Orchards. All morning long, cars and trucks had driven past her cottage to the bunkhouses farther down the road.

Now she was sitting on a bench outside the charming gift shop, a paradise of old-fashioned candies, relishes, teas and jams, as well as embroidered aprons, towels and every ordinary kitchen gadget known to man. A hundred things to tempt visitors.

Elinor, Robert and Susan were moving among the workers, greeting many from last year and introducing themselves to new hires. To her annoyance, Abby found herself searching for Jake, but he was nowhere to be seen. She shrugged. The orchards weren't his job. Maybe he had kid patrol today.

Finally the official welcome began. For the next

two hours, Abby learned about apples and her upcoming day-to-day life—meals, time sheets, hours. The group would start with early Macs, which were to be picked by hand rather than by machine. These apples were slated to be sold as fresh fruit, not used for other products like sauce or juice.

In order to reach the high branches, they would use ladders. Robert indicated a pickup truck loaded with bright yellow painted ladders slowly rolling toward them. The door opened, and Jake jumped down from the driver's seat and waved to the crowd.

He looked good. Very good. An olive-green jersey paired with worn snug jeans on a body that moved with fluidity and grace. Abby's heart shifted into high gear as she absorbed the twinkling blue eyes and the warm smile he bestowed on the crowd. Then those eyes met hers, darkened and moved on, his attention definitely elsewhere.

She swallowed the hurt, annoyed at herself for the feeling. She knew the rules, had agreed with Jake to stick to the job at hand. She concentrated on the orientation again. Everyone was gathering around Jake's truck. She joined the crowd and learned they'd be setting up the ladders in the orchard that day.

She also learned that the Templetons didn't believe in wasting time. Not an hour later, Abby and her younger partner, Lucy Delgado, propped up several ladders along one of their assigned rows of trees and were examining the large canvas bags they'd been given to wear.

"We could be either apple pickers or newspaper carriers," laughed Abby as she examined the bag.

"Ah, the newspapers are better," replied Lucy in her lilting Jamaican accent. "Only one delivery a day! Tomorrow, it's up and down these ladders and fill these bags so much, you'll say, ah, fat Sunday papers are easier."

Lucy's eyes shone as she spoke with the authority of experience. Abby knew the girl wasn't really complaining. She had worked the two past seasons at Templeton Orchards and had obviously returned for a third. "It's hard work, but these people treat you good, real good, like human beings, not like at some places I been. Yes, sirree, this family is a good family."

"Glad to hear you say that, Lucy. It's good to see you again." Jake's voice interrupted.

"Hiya, Mister Jake. It's good to be back."

"You've got a new responsibility this year," said Jake as he nodded at Abby.

Lucy turned toward Abby, a speculative gleam in her eye. "A new partner. That's fine."

"A greenhorn," clarified Jake. "She's never done this before."

"Oh, pooh. There's a first time for everyone. Not to worry. I'll watch out for her."

Abby took two giant steps backward. "If you

want to pretend I'm invisible, I can easily make it a reality." In her own life, she made a point of always including the human subject under discussion *in* the conversation if the person was in the room.

"Now hold on, Abigail," said Jake. "It's my job to check on the new staff and their partners. You're in good hands with Lucy."

"I never had a doubt." She met his gaze and held it. "I think you can continue to the other pairs of new workers. Lucy and I are fine."

His eyebrow arched, but he stayed put. "I'll leave when I'm satisfied with what I see."

Could this cold, business-only Jake be the same person who'd showed such concern about her flash-back yesterday? Her eyes narrowed. Sure it could. She and Jake had no relationship. He'd made it very clear that he and his daughter were off-limits.

She sighed. None of their feelings really mattered at all. Three months of outdoor labor was what she wanted—and what she'd get.

JAKE KISSED STACEY on the forehead that evening as he tucked her into bed. "Good night, baby," he said, spreading the light blanket over her. "I'll take Betsy for a last walk and then turn in."

"But you'll be gone tomorrow."

He hated the thread of worry in her voice, and he hated the guilt he felt. "Don't you like living with Grandma and the family?"

"But you're not here," she whispered, turning away from him.

Her words were better than any valentine card, and his eyes misted. But if he moved her to Boston, she'd have strangers as caregivers for long hours and no Betsy to play with. Not a good life for a little girl.

"In two weeks, I'll be on vacation—right here with you, remember?"

"Yes, but—" Stacey's words were barely audible.

"But what, sweetheart?"

"Doesn't matter." Stacey turned back to face him. "I'm glad Abby's here. I like her."

Great. Just what he didn't need. If Stacey knew Abby was a shrink, she wouldn't like her quite as much. In fact, his daughter would be angry if she thought another therapist was in her life. Jake had promised her no more "talk doctors."

"Abby's going to be working in the orchards all day, Pumpkin."

"I know."

Jake sat at the side of his daughter's bed. "Listen to me, honey." He paused until he had her attention. "Abby has her own reason for being here. She wants to do a job that's different from what she does back home. Remember her sabbatical? She chose to pick apples, something she can do by herself. So try to keep out of her way. Okay?"

The female Templeton blue eyes watered up. "She doesn't like me, does she?" asked Stacey.

"Of course she likes you!" Jake spluttered. "Everyone likes you. Everyone loves you, Pumpkin. You're numero uno around here." But Stacey had turned over on to her stomach, and Jake knew none of his words had penetrated. Why couldn't he talk to his child without screwing up?

He leaned over and kissed his daughter again. "I love you, Stace. I hope you know how much."

Stacey didn't reply.

He left her room in a thoughtful mood, motioned to the dog and walked downstairs with the collie at his side. "You're a good girl, too, Betsy," he said, rubbing her head. "Take care of our Pumpkin during the week for me." He swore the hound understood his every word as she whined back at him and licked his hand. He knew it was nonsense, but felt comforted.

His mom, Robert and Sue were wonderful guardians, but had extra busy lives now. And Sue was not really up to par. She looked peaked, despite the smile on her face. If he didn't miss his guess, she'd be ordered off her feet very soon. He shook his head at the timing, and eyed the dog again. With the twins such a handful, Betsy might prove invaluable with her herding instincts and common sense.

But he supposed the real truth was that it would

be better for everyone if *he* were around more these days. The admission came easily and surprised him. Maybe it was because he'd always enjoyed the harvesting season. Or maybe it was time he handled Stacey himself instead of depending on therapists that didn't work out. Or maybe he wanted to make sure Abby didn't get involved with his daughter. So many reasons to request a third week's vacation. He'd talk to Steve about it tomorrow. His boss was a family man himself.

With the dog at his side, he whistled as he left the house and inhaled the cool night air. The dark sky twinkled with myriad constellations and the moon lit the path ahead of him. He followed it around the back and looked toward Abby's cottage a hundred and fifty feet away. A light shone through the curtains, so she was still up.

For a moment, he was tempted to invite her to walk with him, but finally turned around and chose another path, a solitary one.

ABBY STEPPED BACK from the window, allowing the curtains to fall into place. She hadn't known Jake was outside until she raised the sash, needing to fill her lungs with fresh air after finishing her aerobic routine. And then she'd seen him looking her way, as though undecided about whether to visit. She immediately felt a whole lot better about herself. Too bad that he was so busy protecting everyone—himself included—that he'd forgotten how to live.

Maybe she would remind him.

JAKE STRODE into his office at Mass General early Monday morning, his mind geared to the day ahead. Two new patients, three follow-ups, an angioplasty procedure and an engraved-in-stone meeting with Stephen West, M.D., the team leader for the research Jake was engaged in. Conversations with Steve always sparked ideas and creativity, and although he had no idea of the agenda, Jake looked forward to the meeting. He'd also have an opportunity to ask about extending his vacation.

"Good morning, Connie." Jake held out his hand, palm open, as his ever-competent secretary slapped a bunch of pink message slips into it. "Anything important?"

"According to whom? You or me?" Connie—happily married, mother-of-twins-in-college-at-the-same-time-so-I'll-be-working-until-I'm-a-hundred-and-six—Rogers sat back in her chair eyeing her boss.

Jake looked at the astute, but irreverent, woman who held his working life together with a computer, organizational skills and the diplomatic savvy of a U.N. delegate. Too bad she used the last trait on everyone but him, even on a Monday morning.

"Spit it out, Constance. You look as though you're ready to burst."

"I am! I am!" Her grin said it all. Talk about body language, she was as open and easy to read as the Sunday comics. "That new resident stopped in to see if you had a free minute," she continued. "The cute one—Debbie—with the long blond braid and the long legs to match. Single." She let a pulse beat pass and leaned forward in her chair. "So, what do you think?"

He could have fired the meddling dynamo a thousand times just for her sass. But she was one hundred percent loyal to him and had proved it beyond measure in recent times. "What I think is that you should give me the other messages, the ones that are really important."

"Aw, Jake. She's cute. And smart."

He hated to spoil her fun, but he wasn't interested in blondes. "Messages?"

"Of course. You have another new patient today. I *had* to book her because she's a referral from sweet Mrs. Santana who thinks you walk on water."

He smiled at Connie's description. Sylvia Santana was every doctor's dream patient. She listened carefully, asked questions, answered questions fully and followed instructions to the letter. And now she was enjoying much-improved health after some medical and cardiovascular interventions.

But Connie wasn't finished defending herself yet. "So how could I turn her down when she called you her last hope."

Jake grunted. "That's a little dramatic for me. And I'm sure it's not true."

"She believes it, although she did want to reassure you that she wasn't expecting miracles. Just an appointment."

Miracles! Just what he and Abby had discussed. And here was proof that deep down, every patient expected them. "Anything else I should know about, boss?"

Connie grinned. "Just Dr. West reminding you about your appointment with him at three today."

"I'm looking forward to it."

"Gee whiz! Why can't I see that happy look on your face when I try to fix you up?" Connie complained.

He laughed out loud. Couldn't help it. Connie was so sincere, she was comical with all her good intentions.

"Oh, stop laughing so hard," she protested, waving him away. "I'm worried about you, Jake. It's time to let yourself meet…oh, never mind," she amended. "*You'll* know when it's time."

"Thanks, Con," he said. "It's nice to be treated like a grown-up around here once in a while. Besides," he added with a wink as he walked into his private office, "I like brunettes better."

"Well, okay!" The woman's eyes sparkled. "Let's see, I have a niece…no, too young. My neighbor's daughter…"

Jake was still laughing as he closed the door on her musings. He didn't want anyone arranging dates for him. He didn't have time. He had a daughter at home. And this week, there was someone else there—an intriguing brunette—whom he had to keep tabs on...for Stacey's sake.

At three o'clock that afternoon, Jake's mind was focused only on Dr. West. About ten years older than Jake and equally dedicated to finding methods of avoiding heart surgeries, Stephen West had worked tirelessly to develop the endovascular device program at Mass General. These devices—specialized catheters—corrected problems in blood vessels around the heart and other vital organs of the body. The procedure used to insert them was relatively simple and they offered an alternative to surgery.

Thirty minutes after their meeting started, Jake could only stare in amazement at the offer Dr. West had extended to him. "Lead investigator? The new heart failure intervention project? Myocardial cell delivery?" he repeated.

"Uh, Jake," said Steve West with a straight face, "for an articulate guy, you're sounding a bit like a parrot right now."

A parrot? So what? He was lucky he could still breathe! The offer was an honor. A challenge. A lot to assimilate. And Jake wanted it! Not only was it a boost to his career—at thirty-five, the timing was perfect—but working on a cutting-edge project in the area he'd chosen was a dream come true. He needed a minute.

"You say the funding's all in place?" he asked.

"Almost every penny," replied the older doctor

with a smile. "And more will come as we show results."

"And when would I start?" asked Jake. "What about my patients?"

The more he learned, the more challenging the project became. He would have to assemble a team of investigators, organize the physical lab. Maintain his clinical practice. Extra vacation was obviously out of the question.

But his fingers tingled, his heart pounded, and he fought to control his responses so Steve wouldn't know just how excited he was. Suddenly, an image of Abby flashed through his mind. Abby, with her luscious dark hair, her big chocolate eyes. He wanted to call her and share his news. As a colleague, she'd understand what the project meant to his career. As a woman... Well, that was the problem. She wasn't the woman for him.

ABBY'S FIRST DAY of work at the orchard dawned crystal clear and sunny. Fluffy white clouds dotted the cerulean-blue sky, and a slight chill hung in the morning air. She inhaled deeply, enjoying the fragrance of a New England autumn, so different from the warmer and more humid California air she was used to.

Quickly, however, she detected the aroma of freshly brewed coffee and followed its airborne trail to the large urn outside the gift shop. She filled her cup to the brim, anxious for the jolt of caffeine.

Sleep had come more easily last night, but had only lasted about four hours. She wondered what tonight would bring after a day of hard labor.

"Good morning, Abby," said a familiar feminine voice. "Grab a bagel, too. You'll need some sustenance to get you through the morning."

Abby turned and smiled. Susan Templeton looked more vigorous than she had two nights ago, but Abby noted the strain around her eyes. "Hi there. How are you feeling?"

"I think I'm feeling a lot better than Robert," she laughed. "With all the worrying he does, he might as well be the one carrying this baby." She patted her swollen stomach and looked around. "I love mornings," she continued. "And I love having breakfast outside."

Abby smiled. She stood next to the other woman, enjoying a shared silence until Susan broke it by speaking.

"Would you like me to have the phone in the cottage activated? It's not an extension to the house and has its own number."

"Why, thank you. Yes, I would. Of course, I'll pick up all charges." Worth the convenience of being able to make long-distance calls to California from the cottage. Between the weekly one to her boss, and others to her family, as well as local calls to Aunt Mo, Abby knew the telephone would be a real time-saver.

"I thought you'd feel that way," said Susan. "So if Jake calls you, at least you'll have some privacy."

Abby fought the heat that crept to her cheeks as she faced the other woman. "I'm not expecting Jake to call me. My thought was for easy long distance."

Susan chuckled. "Trust me, he'll call." She stepped closer to Abby. "I know my brother-in-law very well, probably better than he knows himself, and I haven't seen him cast the smallest glance at anyone since Claire died. Except for you."

"Your imagination is working overtime." Abby put her cup down. "I have to go, Susan. Don't want to keep Lucy waiting."

"He's a good guy, Abby," Susan said. "Even though he can be a jerk sometimes. And he worries about Stacey too much. But just give him a chance…"

Abby waved and took off toward her assigned position. Was she paranoid, or was everyone waging a not-so-subtle campaign to match her with Jake? First, Aunt Maureen, and now Susan. She almost laughed at the absurdity. If these well-meaning matchmakers knew of her promise to keep away from Stacey, they wouldn't have dared to broach their ideas.

By three o'clock that afternoon, Jake was the furthest item in her thoughts. *Shoulders.* That's all she could think of. Her shoulders. Aches. Pains. She'd lost count of the times she climbed up and down the ladder, filling her canvas bag and emptying it into the large crates that stood between the rows of trees, or the times she readjusted the ladder to reach the apples at the top, the ones closest to the sun.

She looked at her partner and sighed. Lucy hadn't emitted even one moan. Not one. And had picked at least twenty-five percent more apples than Abby. Oh, well. It wasn't *her* first time! Abby enjoyed working with Lucy. She had tales to tell in her musical voice, tales of her annual trips up north to harvest strawberries in June, vegetables through the summer, and apples in the fall. Lucy made the stories interesting and amusing, but Abby knew that migrant workers often labored under less-than-appealing conditions. But not at Templeton Orchards. Somehow, the thought comforted.

By five o'clock that afternoon, Abby's reality was a hot bath, followed by two aspirin and an early dinner alone in the cottage. Disappointed that her regular aerobic workouts had done almost nothing to prepare her for outdoor labor, she practically hobbled to bed and collapsed, her eyes closing immediately.

She would have loved a massage.

She needed a massage. Behind her eyelids, she dreamed of a whole-body, head-to-toe, deep, intense rubdown. She longed for strong hands to knead her back muscles. Hands to travel up her spine. Down her spine. Competent hands circling her shoulders. Special attention to her thighs, calves. Jake's hands,

strong and competent, paying attention to every
nook and cranny...

She shivered with heat and kicked off the covers.
She wanted to kick her traitorous mind. Sexual flings
were not her style, and from what she could ascer-
tain, not Jake's either. A genuine relationship with
Jake would be almost too complicated to consider.
Too many emotions and people at risk. It couldn't
lead anywhere.

She clicked on the bedside lamp and glanced at
her selection of paperbacks on the night table. A
complex mystery should do it. She'd choose romance when she was back in California developing
a social life.

CHAPTER SIX

THE SHRILL RING of the phone woke her up. Abby blinked in the lamplight, looked down at the paperback lying on her bed and checked the clock radio on the night table. Two hours had passed since she'd lain down and it was only nine o'clock! She reached for the phone and groaned out loud. Her muscles felt worse now than they had earlier. How would she ever climb a ladder tomorrow?

"Hello," she whispered, mentally giving points to Susan and the phone company for fast action.

"Abby? Is that you?" Jake's voice.

"Sort of, as long as I don't have to move my arms or legs."

"Your arms or...? Oh, hell! This is exactly why I called. The new staff in the bunkhouses quit early today and so should you have. Why didn't Lucy insist? My brother has a lot to answer for. Okay, Ms. Moan-and-Groan, how bad is it?"

Wow, he was upset. But why? Charley horse wasn't life or death. But maybe he considered her an informal patient if the greenhorns were his responsibility. She ignored the anger and focused on the concern. "Uh…you don't want to know."

"Try me."

"Okay," she replied slowly. "Let's just say that if the cottage was on fire, I'd wait to be rescued and hope for the best."

A long, low whistle came through the phone line. "That bad?" he replied. "Poor girl. Listen up. Stay where you are and don't move. You'll be getting company in a few minutes, and I'll be calling back."

Click. He'd disconnected. Abby looked at the phone in her hand. Don't move? Had he just told her not to move? He had to be kidding. A grin crossed her face. The organized, intelligent, commonsense guy who wanted no part of her wasn't making much sense at all. Because of her.

Before she could think too much about it, however, a knock on the door was accompanied by a shouted greeting. "Abby! It's Robert and Lucy. We're coming in."

The cavalry had arrived. Jake worked fast. A man of action as well as thought. "I'll be right there," she called, swinging her legs over the bed, preparing to greet her visitors.

She needn't have bothered.

"Stay where you are," said Robert, echoing Jake's order. He crossed to the bedroom doorway and held up a brown bottle. "We're all following doctor's orders here. Lie still and let Lucy work some magic with this stuff.''

Lucy waved at her from behind Robert's tall frame.

Abby offered a tiny smile, then turned to Robert. ''Just what is that 'stuff' you're toting? Horse liniment?''

Robert laughed, his eyes sparkling, and Abby could see images of Jake superimposed there.

''Not exactly 'horse' medicine, but close,'' he replied. ''All you need to know is that it does the job.''

''And I'll feel human again?''

''Absolutely,'' he assured her as the phone rang.

Abby began reaching for the receiver behind her, but Robert dashed for it, and all she was privy to was a one-sided conversation.

''Yes, Lucy's with me. She'll rub her down.... No, I don't abuse the help.... She could have quit early....'' Robert winked and looked imploringly at her. ''Abby, tell him I announced it at the orientation, will you? He thinks I'm a—now, what did he call me—an insensitive jerk with no thought for anyone but myself and I should have especially looked out for greenhorns. Tell him, Abby,'' Robert repeated in a mock display of despair as he handed her the phone.

''You're being too hard on him, Jake,'' laughed

Abby. "He did warn us to take it easy, but I guess I was too stubborn to quit."

"Well, don't make the same mistake tomorrow," Jake said. "Start late, leave early. And that's doctor's orders."

"Now there's a business philosophy that'll earn megabucks for me and Templeton Orchards." Despite her sore muscles and his scolding, Abby grabbed the opportunity to tease Jake. "Besides, won't that bottle Lucy's holding cure me by tomorrow? Maybe I'll be ready to work a double shift!"

She had to hold the phone away from her ear as Jake exploded, but she couldn't stop grinning. The doctor wasn't used to someone disobeying orders. And for a woman who'd been racked with grief and stress for weeks, she felt totally relaxed at the moment. A couple of interesting observations which she tucked into the back of her mind.

She cautiously returned the receiver to her ear. "Just kidding, Jake. No double shifts. Yes, your brother's still here."

Robert interrupted her. "Tell him I'm leaving now so Lucy can give you a good rubdown." Suiting action to words, Robert strode out of the cottage, admonishing Lucy to call him when she'd finished her work if she wanted an escort back to the bunkhouse.

"Hang on, Jake," said Abby into the phone. "I've got to turn over."

PERSPIRATION BEADED Jake's lip. Turn over? Back to front? Front to back? Abby was a beautiful woman with a beautiful body. He could picture her in both positions as clearly as if he were in the cottage. He wished he were.

"Lucy needs to work over every muscle," he growled into the receiver. "From feet to neck...pressing deep and hard." A rivulet of sweat ran from his temple as his body stirred.

Why was he torturing himself like this? Abby was sort of a patient right now, not a woman! What was he thinking? Of course she was a woman. But not in his life. He covered the speaker to muffle his groan.

"Jake! This stuff stinks! Yuck."

Abby's indignation startled him as he pictured the serious psychologist wrinkling her nose. His body relaxed, and in his apartment he leaned back in his chair and propped his feet on the desk in front of him. Impossible to continue a fantasy when the woman in his dream says "Yuck."

"Stinky is a small price for the relief you're going to feel."

"Ahhh, you may be right. Lucy, that's so good. Oh, my calves. Lucy, you're the best. Oh, yes!"

Her voice oozed satisfaction with her massage, and Jake's heat returned tenfold. Calves, thighs—his mind wandered, suddenly undisciplined, remembering all the parts of the female anatomy that he hadn't allowed himself to recall in years. The joy of making love.

He cleared his throat. "I'll call you tomorrow night, Abby. Quit early. Doctor's orders."

"Sometimes, Jake," came the husky voice from the cottage, "you can be very sweet. Very nice." The voice paused. "And now I'll say good-night... and thanks."

The line disconnected and he stared at the receiver in his hand. *Sweet.* What kind of word was that for a woman to use on a robust all-American male? And *nice.* A bland word for sure. But she'd meant them as compliments. He'd bet his last dollar on that. Compliments from an attractive, intelligent—make that a usually intelligent—woman.

Maybe Connie wasn't wrong today. Maybe it was time to go forward with relationships. Abby certainly had caught his attention. No question about it. And yet... and yet the past clung to him like a remembered dream. How could his darling Claire rest in peace when the husband she'd loved had let her down? How could she rest in peace when the daughter she'd loved with all her heart couldn't find peace in her life? How could Jake even think about moving forward when he still had to fix the past? He was the only parent left to do it, and so help him God, he would.

Nothing had changed. Stacey had to come first.

ABBY BOUNCED out of bed Tuesday morning and hummed to herself as she prepared for the day. Lucy's deep-heat potion seemed to have worked its magic. She stretched her arms, twisted her torso, then lunged left and right. Almost pain-free. She glanced at the clock, grabbed a piece of bread and ran outside. No wonder she felt great. She'd overslept.

She loped across the road toward the orchards, almost crashing into the twins.

"Hi, Abby."

"Hi, Abby."

She had to get used to listening in stereo when chatting with these kids. "Hi, boys. Where are you going today?"

"We're going to take care of the baby aminals."

"Yeah. That's our job."

"And where's your cousin?"

"Oh, Stacey's helping Mommy." Jon's comment. At least Abby thought it was Jon.

"Yeah," said Mac, nodding his head, all serious now. "Stacey doesn't have a mommy anymore, so she shares our mommy."

Jon nodded along with his brother, then leaned in closer to whisper, "Stacey's mommy's in heaven, and you know how *that* works."

Abby shook her head, fascinated.

"Once you get to heaven," Jon continued, "you

have to stay there. So Auntie Claire's in heaven and Stacey's here. And Stacey's sad all the time.''

Mac chimed in again. ''But Grandma says we're lucky Stacey's not in heaven, too.''

''Yeah,'' agreed Jon. ''We're lucky 'cause then Uncle Jake would be too, too sad.''

''And Grandma, too,'' said Mac.

''Oh, yeah. And you know what else?'' asked Jon.

Abby shook her head, having absolutely no idea where this conversation was going.

But evidently, Jon did. ''I like being happy better,'' he added.

''Me, too,'' replied Mac. ''Happy's better than sad.''

Abby's jaw almost hit her feet. Were these kids only six years old? And how had one ''Hi, boys,'' evolved into a poignant report on the status of the family? Not that Abby hadn't known about Claire and the accident, but the boys' personal take on the subject tore a piece of her heart. Jon and Mac might be imps of the highest order, but they were loving, sweet imps.

''Tell your mom and Stacey hi from me. Maybe if you gave them some kisses, you'd make them feel better.''

The boys' round eyes grew to dinner-plate size. ''Kisses? Yuck!''

''Yuck!''

As though choreographed, the twins turned on their heels and ran toward the petting zoo. Abby watched them go, caught between laughter and tears. If they'd been her boys, she'd have kissed them until they begged for relief.

And Stacey? She shook her head as she once again walked toward her assigned section of early Macs. Not fair to compare the children. The twins' world hadn't been ripped apart the way their cousin's had. Abby winced thinking about Stacey's pain. Would anyone be able to help the girl put her world back together?

FROM HIS BOSTON APARTMENT, Jake reached for the phone that evening, wanting to speak with Stacey as usual and eager to check up on Abby. Maybe he'd tell her his big news about the research appointment. He dialed her number at the cottage.

Her voice was light, full of laughter, and he settled back in his chair. "You sound great for a lady who couldn't move last night."

"I feel great. Bet I could even keep up with the twins."

"I wouldn't bet real money if I were you," Jake replied.

"Well, after seeing them in action, I wouldn't either," Abby said, "but in general it was a good day. And in case you're wondering, I've only seen your daughter from a distance."

Ouch. The reminder pinched but he chose to ignore it. "Um...I've called about something else, actually two things."

"Oh?"

He couldn't miss the touch of defensiveness, could almost feel her bracing herself and suddenly he felt like a heel. And awkward, to boot. He'd been so sure of himself minutes ago. What had happened? "Just as a friend," he began, "not a doctor, I'm wondering if you've had any more flashbacks?"

"No, thank God," came the instant reply. "I have to call Martin tomorrow and update him."

"Ah-ha. You're under care."

He heard the pause before she replied in a harder voice. "Yes. Yes, I am. Any problem with that?"

"Problem? Not at all, Abby. Actually, I'm relieved. Sometimes physicians need help to heal themselves. Remember?"

"I keep telling you, Jake, I'm not that kind of doctor."

"And I keep telling you, your professional goal is the same as any medical doctor's. Help your patients get better."

Another pause prefaced her quiet "Thank you. That means a lot to me."

"You're welcome." A heartbeat passed and in that moment Jake felt they weren't strangers.

"And what's the second item on your list?"

Her voice got him back on track. He'd known

he'd be excited talking about the research project for the first time, but he found himself going on and on. A full blue streak. About Steve West, about the new lab, about new possibilities for patients.

"That's fantastic, Jake," said Abby when he was done. "Just fantastic. To be recognized by your peers like that. You get to keep your patients and research the projects you believe in. It's a huge boost for your career. What more could you want, except maybe…time?"

Her reaction was everything he thought it would be, except for that last comment. "Time? I already put in more time than anyone should expect."

"And will this project add to it?"

"I'm rearranging. Giving up my teaching at the medical school."

"Teaching? I didn't know you did that."

"Only one night a week at Harvard and I enjoy it, but the research is more important to me."

"Want a word of advice from a plain old therapist?"

He chuckled. "You're not plain and you're not old," he replied. "Moreover, I can always use advice." And discard it immediately if he wanted to.

"The important thing is, Jake," Abby continued, "that your time with Stacey remains constant. You can't shortchange her."

"I agree. But why would you think I'd do that?

Do I seem like such an unconcerned father?'' Her insinuation hurt, more than he would have thought.

"Not at all! I think you're very concerned. But maybe, in all the excitement, you haven't considered the weekends.''

"I have,'' he said. "A few Saturdays may be taken up in the beginning, but after that, we should have rotating assignments.''

"Okay,'' said Abby. "It's your call.''

"And you don't approve.''

"Not for me to say one way or the other. All I know is that Stacey needs consistency in her life. And she's looking to you to give it to her.''

Did she think he didn't know that? "I'll be back Friday night. As usual. Stacey and I will have this weekend together. In fact, we have a shopping date because school starts next week. And the week after that, I start my vacation and will be at the orchards for two weeks. I know she's looking forward to my being there.''

"She'll love it.''

"And you?'' The question popped out of his mouth without thought. He pictured her big brown eyes and sexy smile, and his heart kaboomed while waiting for her answer.

"I think I can handle it,'' she replied.

"Good. That's good.'' He felt himself relax and said good-night, then glanced at his watch and called his daughter. Damn! For the first time in two years he was ten minutes late. He should have called Stacey first.

ABBY MEANDERED toward her cottage Wednesday evening, enjoying the lingering rays of the sun, appreciating the landscape of rolling hills surrounding the orchard. Her co-workers were also making their way to their homes-away-from-home, some heading for the bunkhouses on the property, others seeking their own trailers, while some locals climbed into their vehicles for the short trip home.

In the near distance, she spotted two identical blond heads chasing a ball. Funny how she always seemed to be running into the twins, but rarely managed to bump into Stacey. Only once in the last three days had the child waved at her before skipping off. During the same time, Abby had chatted regularly with Robert, Susan and Elinor, but never with Jake's daughter. For a moment, she wondered if he'd forbidden the child to connect with her, but then dismissed the thought as unworthy. Maybe it was just as well, she thought, since she'd given her own word not to encourage a friendship.

She sniffed the air as she walked toward home, identifying the hearty aroma of Italian sauce, but deciding to abstain from the nightly communal dinner offered by the Templetons to their workers. Just like breakfast, dinner was served informal buffet style with long tables and benches arranged to accommodate everyone.

But tonight, Abby wanted to be on her own, to reestablish her regular aerobic routine before partaking of any meal. Picking apples offered exercise, fresh air and sunshine, but she missed the music and the disciplined whole-body workout that her tapes and CDs provided. And afterward, her own groceries and a hot shower would sustain her. She'd end her day with a call to Martin and then hopefully fall into a wholesome, undisturbed sleep that would last the night.

She let herself into the cottage and closed the door behind her, enjoying the quiet and privacy of her own space. She leaned against the door and surveyed the surroundings. She felt happy here. As happy as she could have hoped to be in such a short time. The positive thought prompted her to call Martin right then, earlier than planned. A good decision, she thought as she dialed the phone. With the three-hour time difference, she'd reach her supervisor in the office instead of at home and that could only be a bonus for him. Ten minutes later, she was glad she had. With words of cautious encouragement and gentle questions about her experiences and about her flashback, Martin managed to probe her activities and her feelings. She knew she sounded much more relaxed than when she'd left and he seemed satisfied that this time-out-of-time would be good for her, would help her to heal.

"So keep up the apple picking if that's what it takes and keep writing your journal," he joked. "But tell that guy Jake that I expect you back in California before too long!"

She almost dropped the phone. Had she spoken about Jake that much? Her mind raced over her conversation as she said goodbye, and she had to admit that she probably had. Jake was with her when she'd had her flashback; he was part of the orchard-owning family; he was a single dad with child problems. And he'd all but asked her on the phone if she'd spend some time with him on his vacation. She'd mentioned all of that to Martin. Next week she'd keep her mouth shut.

Now she changed into stretch shorts and an exercise bra, went into the living room and selected her music. She felt a slight breeze through the window and welcomed it.

Warm-up first, low impact, but she wanted the music loud. She hummed along as she worked each part of her body, enjoying the familiarity of getting back into her routine. Her muscles warmed and loosened, she felt a grin cross her face. Yes! This was more like it!

Except for the high-pitched sound coming through the open window. Abby twirled around, picked up the beat again, and stared at the two shadows behind the sheer curtains on the other side of the screened window. One shadow had pointed ears and a snout to match, a snout that was now lifted in song or in protest. Giggles rose in her chest and almost erupted until she saw the other shadow moving to the music, right on the beat—the other shadow was copying Abby's every move.

Instincts alert, Abby said nothing, just continued to face Stacey and lead the routine. She couldn't see the girl clearly, just as she was sure Stacey couldn't see her clearly, but Abby wanted the child to stay. Despite Jake's request. This was the first time Stacey had approached Abby and there had to be a reason.

"Now, we'll do a grapevine step…to the right," Abby cued. "Like this. Side, back, side, front. And back to the left. Side, back, side, front. Again. Good job."

Abby grapevined closer to the screened window and without missing a step, gently pulled the curtain to the side. "Would you like to join me, Stacey? You and Betsy are welcome here."

But Stacey came to a dead stop in the exercise, a look of horror on her face, and for a moment Abby was frightened. What was going on in the mind of this child? There was no obvious reason for fear.

Abby backpedaled. "You don't have to come in, honey. It's okay." She would have loved to turn off the music, but couldn't reach the player and stay with Stacey at the same time. "We can still practice like this."

But Stacey backed away, one step at a time, shaking her head, not saying a word.

Abby stood quietly, watching the girl and her companion make their way to the big house. There was no question in Abby's mind that the child had problems beyond grief for her mother. With normal grieving, people did return to their regular activities despite the sadness. Stacey, however, was running away from everything—from school, from other children, even from her father.

And now she was running from Abby.

CHAPTER SEVEN

STACEY PUT her hands on her hips and stared defiantly at her grandmother. "I don't care if he's coming home late. I want to have supper with him."

"I said you can wait up, honey, but you need to eat with the rest of us."

"But—"

"Stace," her uncle Robert cut in. "That's enough."

Ooh! These grown-ups never understood anything. Her dad needed Stacey because he'd been alone all week in Boston. If she didn't keep him company tonight, he'd be alone again because everyone else would have finished their dinner before he arrived. But Grandma wanted Stacey to eat with the family. She always worried about Stacey's appetite and wouldn't want her to miss a meal. Suddenly Stacey had a great idea.

"Gram," she said. "Here's the deal. I'll have a peanut-butter-and-jelly sandwich with you, and then I'll eat dinner with Daddy." There. She'd figured out a solution to make everybody happy.

"Almost a deal, Stacey," said Elinor. "How about if you eat dinner with us and have a PBJ with Daddy? Then you won't fall asleep with your head in the soup."

Stacey giggled. Sometimes Grandma was funny. And Uncle Robert was usually great. But she really wanted her dad.

"Okay," she agreed because she knew she couldn't win. She was nine years old, ignorant about a lot of things, but she wasn't stupid. She knew when to give in so she could win a bigger fight another time. And she didn't actually *lose*. At least she got to stay up late and keep her dad company while he ate. Maybe if everyone else went to bed, she and Daddy could be alone. That would be great, but what could they safely talk about?

She thought about that question a few hours later as she sat on the front porch with Betsy. No book to distract her this time; it was too dark to read outside. She wore a sweatshirt because the evenings were getting chillier.

"School weather," she said to the collie who was lying with her head on Stacey's lap. She stroked the back of the dog's neck, scratched behind her ears and smiled when Betsy snuffed with pleasure. She loved Betsy and she loved making Betsy happy.

She wished she could make her dad happy.

Suddenly tears filled her eyes. Something was wrong with her. Everyone knew it. That's why

Daddy kept taking her to all those different doctors. The talking doctors.

Everyone was right. Something *was* very wrong with her, but only she knew what it was. And she couldn't tell anybody, doctors or family. Because if Daddy found out the secret, he would never forgive her. He'd stop loving her, maybe even hate her.... Oh, God. What would she do if he didn't want her anymore? Why, oh, why had she nagged her mom to drive that day? If only they hadn't gone out in the snow. And there was more. But she never could quite remember the rest of what happened. The only thing she knew for sure was that she missed her mom and all the happy times.

Tears rolled down her cheeks and she quickly wiped them away with the back of her hands, then put her head in her lap. Everything was such a mess. And she had to figure out a way to fix it.

An engine disturbed the quiet of the night, and seconds later headlights cut through the darkness. Stacey jumped to her feet, almost knocking Betsy off the porch. She wiped her face one last time and peered at the approaching car. Yup, it was her dad. And he was waving to her and smiling.

Instantly, she felt better. At least for the moment. Her stomach didn't jump the way it usually did when she thought about the past. She waved back at her dad and waited for him to reach her.

"HI, PUMPKIN," called Jake as he slammed the car door behind him and walked toward his daughter. He always moved slowly when he first saw Stacey after an absence, wanting to give her the chance to run to him. He usually waited in vain. To his disappointment, tonight was no exception.

He instantly decided to change tactics. He covered the last steps quickly and reached for his daughter. "Ready?" he asked. Without waiting for a reply, he scooped her up and twirled her around. She squealed and clung to him in the way that every father savored. He was her protector, her hero. At least for the moment. And he loved it!

He slowed the turns but didn't release her. Why quit when he was ahead? He held her in his arms as he walked into the house, gratified that she didn't squirm to get down.

He entered an empty kitchen, glanced at the clock and said, "Everyone must have hit the sack already."

"Not quite, Jake," replied Robert, walking in from the hall, grinning when he spotted Stacey in Jake's arms. "Had to check up on my best girl here."

"*Your* best girl," cried Jake in mock anger. "She's *my* best girl. Soon you'll have a gorgeous girl of your own."

"We hope so."

Robert's voice sounded carefully controlled to Jake, and he raised an eyebrow. "Anything new?"

"More precautions. Not to worry about now. Not when you're on a date with my favorite lady."

"Hope Susan doesn't hear you talk like this," said Jake.

"Oh, Daddy!" Stacey interrupted. "Aunt Susan won't care. She's a grown-up and she's so pretty and Uncle Robert loves her so much...just like...just like..." Her breath came in gasps.

"It's okay, sweetheart." Jake stroked her back gently, patted her shoulder and kissed her cheek. "Like who, Stace?" he encouraged. "Tell me what you were going to say."

But Stacey shook her head.

Robert intervened. "Your daughter's been waiting all night for a dinner date with you."

"She has?"

"You bet. She fought the Ogre Elinor for permission to stay up late and won. Your girl's fierce, Jake. A real fighter. I'd be afraid to turn my back if I were you."

"Oh, Uncle Robert," Stacey said, looking from her uncle to her dad. "You're crazy. This whole family is crazy!"

Jake chuckled and kissed Stacey on the cheek, forehead and neck, everywhere he could reach, before carefully lowering her to the floor. If his daughter had tripped over a critical emotion a minute ago, she showed no sign of it now. In fact, their conversation was very normal. Very family. For a brief time, they'd had fun. And it felt so good to him.

"I'm turning in," said Robert. "Stacey knows how to prepare your dinner, right, honey?"

"Sure. Put the plate in the microwave for two minutes."

"An awesome cook," replied Robert as he left the kitchen.

And then Jake was alone with his daughter again. Stacey went to the refrigerator, pulling out a dinner plate loaded with meat loaf, mashed potatoes and snap green beans. He watched her carefully place it on the counter beside the microwave, uncover it and put it in the oven to reheat. It seemed she truly wanted to share time with him. Satisfaction coursed through his blood. So far, he was looking at a great Labor Day weekend.

A vision of Abby flashed through his mind. If she was still up, maybe he'd ask her to walk the dog with him. An innocent request, a great opportunity to get together.

"So, Stace. Are you ready for school next Wednesday?"

Her face drooped, and he could have kicked himself for choosing that topic. Tomorrow was soon enough.

"Let's talk about something good," she replied.

"Okay. What kind of crowds are we expecting Sunday?"

And she was off. She gave him a rundown of the orchard's daily activity this past week. He could always count on the family business to provide a topic of conversation for them. The only topic Stacey had any enthusiasm for. "And tomorrow I'm supervising the cider house," she added.

"Supervising?" Jake raised his eyebrow as he finished the last piece of meat loaf. "What's Harry Lederman going to do if you're supervising?" he asked, referring to the retired state trooper who'd been working the cider house operation for the last four years.

"Well, Mr. Lederman needs my help," protested Stacey. "He said so."

"Thank goodness," replied Jake with a wink. "You had me worried for a minute. I thought you were putting Harry out of a job."

Her expression was priceless. "Daddy, you are so silly. How could I run the cider house when I have to go to school during the day?"

At least she'd accepted that attending school was mandatory. It would be nice if she could like it, of course. Smart as she was, she should love it. Perhaps she just needed more time.

Tonight, he was hopeful about many things.

And now he'd ask the question that had been in

the back of his mind all evening. "See much of Abby during the week, Stace?"

Myriad expressions crossed her face, surprising him with their intensity. An eager smile, a thoughtful reflection, and then a flash of fear. Startled, he almost pulled her into his lap, but then checked himself. He needed more information and he wouldn't get it by scaring his daughter. Forcing himself to relax and wait, he was soon rewarded.

"Only once," replied Stacey, averting her eyes. "And I didn't bother her, Daddy. Anyway, she doesn't always have dinner with everybody outside at the tables, so I couldn't see her even if I wanted to. I think she cooks in the cottage and…and does other things."

No question that his daughter was hiding something. What "other things" could she be referring to? Before he could probe, however, Stacey made a production of clearing his plate and putting it in the dishwasher. Then she turned to him with a brilliant smile.

"I'm so glad you're here. I can't wait for you to be on vacation." She walked toward him and wrapped her arms around his waist.

Thank you, God. He bent down and kissed the top of her head. He'd never give up on this child!

HALF AN HOUR LATER, Jake made his way out of the darkened house through the kitchen door and gazed at Abby's cottage. Only the porch light was on. Maybe she was already asleep like the rest of his family, including Stacey, who'd fallen asleep the moment he'd tucked her into bed. Country life seemed to knock everybody out. He chuckled, quietly comparing the number of hours he put in to the hours his brother put in. They both pulled long shifts, no doubt about it. But the fresh air of the outdoors had Robert hitting the pillow a lot sooner than Jake.

Clouds dotted the night sky and only allowed the moon to light his way for a moment as he crossed the lawn to the long driveway leading to Abby's place. As he looked ahead, he realized her car was gone. So she wasn't sleeping. And she was out on dark unfamiliar roads. Great.

He lowered his body into the rocking chair on the small porch and prepared to wait for her. Going to bed right now would be an exercise in tossing and turning, a futile search for sleep.

As he rocked, the tensions of the week relinquished their grip. Between preparing for his new responsibilities, working with the new residents and having Connie change patient appointments, the days seemed a never-ending potpourri of assignments. Knowing he'd be away for two weeks hadn't helped either. He hoped Connie wouldn't have to track him down for any emergencies or neglected administrative tasks while he was on vacation. Then he dismissed the idea. His colleagues were quite competent to handle his patients and his paperwork for a brief time if needed.

His thoughts meandered until he became cognizant of the night world around him. The chorus of insects, the hoot of an owl, the rustle of leaves as a small mammal rushed by. A cacophony of country sounds, as familiar to him as his own face in the mirror. He'd grown up on this piece of land, had planted trees, had helped nurture the orchards as well as the business. But when the time came to choose, after his grandfather died, well...he took off for medical school and had never looked back except to visit. And now he seemed to be here all the time. He and Stacey.

He peered into the darkness, once more concerned about Abby's whereabouts, and had almost decided to go out searching, when he spotted a pair of headlights turning onto the cottage road. He walked to the porch steps and followed the car's progress, heaving a sigh of relief when he recognized her Mazda. Had he been that frightened? He had to admit the answer was yes. He'd had more than enough trouble in his life with women driving on winding roads.

As soon as the car came to a stop, he walked to the driver's door and jerked it open, ready to explain the facts of country roads to Abby. She turned and looked up at him, just as moonlight once again revealed the landscape, revealed her dark eyes framed by cascading waves of hair. A smile played at the corner of her mouth while the light scent of her perfume teased his nostrils.

"Welcome home," she breathed.

And all thoughts of argument left his mind. In fact, he couldn't think at all. He reached for Abby's arm and gently pulled her out of her seat until she stood in front of him.

"Thank you," he replied. Her full lips enticed him; mesmerized him. What would it be like...? He raised his hand, surprised to see it tremble.

What the hell was he doing? He stepped back, momentarily aghast at his thoughts, his actions. Think about Stacey, he told himself. She doesn't need a therapist getting too close.

"Jake?"

"Yes?"

"Did you want something?"

"No. Yes." He was acting like a jerk. "You were driving alone at night on unfamiliar winding roads."

She smiled. "Don't worry. I'm an excellent driver, with acute vision both day and night. I was with Aunt Maureen this evening, at her rehearsal. I've been there enough times to be familiar with the roads. So relax."

He studied her face for a moment before he replied. "All right. I'm beginning to recognize that independent streak, but do me a favor and leave word with the family next time you go out at night. Someone might worry." *Like him.*

"Jake, you're not responsible for me," she said quietly. "I'm an adult who's been taking care of herself for a long time."

"And that's fine. I've been on my own, too," he said, matching her soft tone. "But...you've joined the family for a while, so consider them."

For a moment, he thought she'd argue. But then she looked pensive.

"What?" he prompted.

She stared at him for what seemed like hours before she said, "It's a strange kind of joining when I'm not allowed to speak to Stacey."

She had him there, and for a moment he felt uncomfortable. Then reason kicked in. "I'm sorry about that, Abby, but my request still stands. You need to help yourself before you can help anyone else. Aren't those your words? Isn't that why you're here?"

Her face tightened, her demeanor stiffened. No soft, sultry woman now. "I haven't forgotten it for a moment. But it's too bad you feel that way. I might be able to help your daughter." She turned and climbed the porch steps.

"Good night," said Jake.

"Good night," she replied, letting herself into the small house without turning around.

Jake stood in the dark, eyes on the closed door.

Could he have made a mistake? Had he thrown away a chance to help Stacey?

THE NEXT MORNING, Jake found himself in the middle of the cider house, inhaling the aroma of clean apples and watching his daughter inspect each aspect of the process as though she were, indeed, the supervisor of the entire operation. No shyness here. She dogged Harry Lederman's footsteps. "Do we have the right mix of apples for the cider? It's got to be sweet *and* tart, you know."

"Don't worry, boss," said Harry with a wink at Jake. "It's all under control. The conveyor belt's humming, the staff's here to inspect, wash, chop and press the fruit, and you're here to sell cider to the customers and explain how it all works."

"I wish…I wish," began Stacey.

Alert, Jake waited for her to finish the sentence, but she didn't.

"What do you wish, Pumpkin?"

She turned away then, and all he saw was her ponytail. "You wouldn't understand."

"Try me."

She pivoted and fisted both hands at her sides. "I wish I could just stay home and work with Grandma and Uncle Robert and Mr. Lederman all the time. I wish school didn't start this week. I wish you could be here all the time."

And he'd been naive enough to believe that the

school situation had been put to bed the night before. Now he had to put a positive spin on everything Stacey vocalized. "You're getting the best fourth-grade teacher in the school, Stace. I happen to know that every kid in third grade wanted her and you were one of the lucky ones."

She didn't answer, so he plunged onward.

"How will you go to college and become the best orchard operator if you don't go to fourth grade? Remember what Abby said last week?"

Now she looked right at him, her blue eyes wide. "Yeah," she whispered, "but I'd still rather be home." She turned from him then, and stared at the conveyor machinery as though she'd never seen it before in her life. "Maybe I could just skip a year?"

"Oh, baby. I'm afraid not." What could he come up with to make her happy? Surely he could think of something! And then he did. A truly inspired thought. He squatted in front of her so they were on eye level.

"Stacey, listen up. I have a great idea. It's something that you really, really like to do, something that you've always been so happy doing, and that you're very, very good at."

He'd captured her attention. "How would you like to go to dancing school again? We'll look for a new one right here in Sturbridge and—" He never got to finish the sentence.

"No-o-o," she screamed and dashed out of the building.

Jake scrambled to his feet and took off after her. What was happening now? Why was she afraid of dancing? Where to begin again?

His kid was fast, but he was taller and no slouch in the physical fitness department. He chased her down the dirt road to the parking lot. She seemed to fly, her feet never touching the ground. Then onward toward the main house, where workers were milling about. And then...then...just as he was ready to engulf her in his arms, she crashed! Right into Abby. Right into a member of the profession that hadn't done Stacey any good at all.

"Two years of psychologists," he snarled as he helped both females to their feet, angry at the world and angry at himself for not being able to fix things. "Two years of shrinks," he repeated, "and we're not one step closer to normalcy."

He lifted Stacey into his arms, her body trembling, his own insides shaking. "Damn it, Abby, why can't I make her better? Happy? With all my schooling, with all my experience, I should be able to figure it out, because there's no one who loves her more than I do."

Abby's hand on his arm burned with the force of the sun. Her five-finger imprint would surely remain for a while. But her voice was soft.

"Jake, Jake," she murmured. "You can help her, but you can't do it for her."

"She's only nine years old!"

"I know. She needs to know you're there for her. But love is not enough. In fact, sometimes it's too much. Stacey needs to do the work herself."

Was Abby for real? How could love not be enough? Without love, they wouldn't have a family. They'd have nothing!

"Uh, thanks for your advice. But right now I think Stacey and I will go school shopping. What do you think, Pumpkin?"

His daughter's quiet "okay" relieved his mind for the moment. "It'll be fun," he continued. "A special father-daughter day for us."

He glanced at Abby, but she was in shrink mode. Her expression gave nothing away. Then she smiled briefly. "Have a good time on your special day."

"Thanks," he said. "And thanks for trying." He lowered Stacey to the ground and took her hand. "Ready to go?"

Stacey nodded and pulled him forward. Maybe a female activity like shopping would pick up her spirits. He shrugged and turned back to Abby.

"Don't work too hard today."

"Sure."

He waved and continued walking. Then turned once more.

Abby remained where she was, a deep furrow lining her forehead, her eyes narrowed. And in her expression this time, he saw concern. For him and Stacey.

CHAPTER EIGHT

THE PHONE RANG that evening just as Abby let herself into the cottage at the end of her workday. Road dust marked her sneakers, perspiration had settled at the nape of her neck. She gathered her hair and held it aloft wondering why she hadn't brushed it into a Stacey-like ponytail that morning. Now she thought about a refreshing shower as she absently picked up the receiver with her other hand.

"Hello, Abby. It's Elinor and I'm inviting you to have dinner with us tonight—if you can put up with the Templeton crew and all our noise."

Abby smiled. "Noise is no problem, but I don't want to intrude. Please don't feel you're responsible for me—"

Elinor interrupted. "Nonsense. We'd love to have you."

Maybe Elinor would love to have her, but Abby doubted Jake would feel the same. "Thank you, then," said Abby. "Count on me for cleanup."

Thirty minutes later, in navy slacks and sweater, Abby opened her front door and found Jake sitting on the steps, flashlight in hand. The porch's overhead light cast interesting shadows on the planes of his face, and his normally bright blue eyes were now dark, intriguing. She could have stared at him for hours. Instead, she waved her own flashlight.

"I don't need an escort anymore."

"No problem." He rose to his feet, his eyes barely blinking as he looked at her. "Pretty woman," he added softly.

Heat rose to her face, and she walked down the steps, away from the light.

"So, how was your shopping trip, if you don't mind my asking?"

"It was typical Stacey," he replied. "She knew exactly what stores she wanted to visit, exactly which styles she wanted, and what colors as well. You're a woman. Take a look tonight and tell me what you think."

"I haven't been nine years old in a long time," Abby said. "Besides, it doesn't matter what I think. Stacey probably knows what's in, what the other kids are wearing. The secret, Jake, is to look like everyone else in school, so you don't stand out. That's the way it works with girls."

"Gee, it's easier to be a boy. Jeans and jerseys. All done."

"And so unique, so individual...so like a group of preadolescents."

His quiet laughter caused a shiver to run through

her, a delicious shiver of possibilities. His intimate tone was inviting and relaxed, sharing her small joke like old friends. Strange, when in reality they were barely friends. She really had to remember that or she could be headed for a fall.

In minutes, Abby was sitting at the familiar table in the country-style kitchen while Jake tossed the salad.

"I hope Elinor warned you about leftovers on Saturday," said Susan as she dished out reheated meatballs and sauce over freshly boiled spaghetti.

"No, I didn't," said Jake's mom from her position at the sink. "Our leftovers are usually better than the first time around."

"Everything smells wonderful." Abby studied Susan Templeton, glad to note she was up and about more these days. But she moved carefully. Five minutes earlier, she hadn't lifted the pot of meatballs to pour them into the serving bowl, but scooped the meat out instead, brushing aside Abby's offer to help. "Next time," she promised. "You're still a guest."

"If this guest can climb trees, she can also help in the kitchen," Abby replied. She rose from her chair, retrieved the large bowl and brought it to the table, which Stacey had set. She could hear the twins' excited voices in the next room and wondered for the hundredth time if their motors ever wore down.

Then Robert returned from the orchards, greeting her as though he hadn't seen her in years.

"I like being surrounded by beautiful women," he said before kissing his wife.

"This guy always knows the right words and the right action," replied Susan, her hand remaining in her husband's much larger one.

Abby smiled. The couple had a good marriage. Nice. She glanced at Jake and caught him staring at her, a thoughtful expression on his face.

"I hope you're not black-and-blue after this morning's collision," he said.

"I'm tougher than that," Abby replied. "Stacey had other things on her mind." She looked at the youngster. "So, did you have a good day with your dad?"

The child nodded. "Yes."

"What did you buy? Dresses or jeans?" Abby gave a hundred percent of her attention to the girl. *Come on, sweetheart, talk to me.*

Stacey remained quiet for a moment, then wrinkled her nose. "Dresses? No way! I got lots of fleece, and sweats, and jeans, and new boots and sneakers." She paused, her expression intent. "Oh, one more thing. A snowsuit." She wrinkled her nose again. "Daddy made me buy it."

Made her? She didn't sound happy. "But doesn't it snow a lot in Massachusetts?"

"Yes, but I wanted a black one and he made me buy pink and purple."

"Oh." Abby would probably have done the same.

Jake jumped into the conversation. "The one we got is colorful. It's beautiful on her." He turned to his daughter. "Stace, admit it. You liked it when you looked in the mirror."

Stacey shrugged.

"I'd love to see what's popular in fourth grade," said Abby. "How about a fashion show after dinner? You can show off like a real model."

Stacey studied her for a moment, uncertainty in her expression, and at first, Abby didn't think the child would cooperate. But then her forehead cleared and a small smile tipped the corner of her mouth. "Okay," she said. "I'll pretend to be a model and I'll pretend these clothes are for other customers who have to go to school next week."

Abby held on to her own smile. She'd settle for one step at a time. "That's fine, honey," she replied, motioning Jake to keep quiet. Surprisingly, he complied.

"So," said Susan. "Dinner first and then a fashion show. Can't think of anything I'd rather do this evening with my family."

"Mom?" said Jonathan with horror in his voice. "Do we have to try on our jeans, too?"

"Well," continued Susan, eyes twinkling, "Uncle Jake bought you each three sets of jeans with jerseys and two sets of corduroys. What do you think?"

"No," replied Mac with certainty. "Boys don't do fashion shows!" He turned to Robert. "Right, Daddy?"

Robert's whoops pervaded the entire room. "Right. Not unless you want to." He turned to his niece then, "But we'll all have eyes on you, gorgeous."

Stacey blushed and giggled just like any little girl would have done. And Abby's hopes ran high. Underneath all the fear and hiding, a sweet, normal little girl lurked. The challenge was to find a way to reach her.

"Gorgeous?" repeated Jake, embracing Stacey and kissing her forehead. "She sure is!"

BUT STACEY would have been more gorgeous if she had chosen colors other than black, charcoal gray or dark brown. Abby said nothing, but was secretly glad when one navy-blue fleece top showed off the little girl's eyes and saved the day. Everyone in the family cheered and clapped as Stacey appeared in each outfit, no matter what the color.

Jake sang "Thank Heaven for Little Girls"—off-key—every time she walked down the stairs. Stacey giggled, and for a half an hour or so, smiled and basked in the approval of her family.

Abby relaxed and joined in, exclaiming over the

The Harlequin Reader Service® — Here's how it works:

NO POSTAGE
NECESSARY
IF MAILED
IN THE
UNITED STATES

BUSINESS REPLY MAIL

FIRST-CLASS MAIL   PERMIT NO. 717-003   BUFFALO, NY

POSTAGE WILL BE PAID BY ADDRESSEE

HARLEQUIN READER SERVICE
3010 WALDEN AVE
PO BOX 1867
BUFFALO NY 14240-9952

Do You Have the LUCKY KEY?

PLAY THE
Lucky Key Game

and you can get

FREE BOOKS
and a **FREE GIFT!**

Scratch the gold areas with a coin. Then check below to see the books and gift you can get!

YES!
I have scratched off the gold areas. Please send me the 2 FREE BOOKS and GIFT for which I qualify. I understand I am under no obligation to purchase any books, as explained on the back of this card.

336 HDL DNVY   135 HDL DNVN

FIRST NAME	LAST NAME

ADDRESS

APT.#	CITY

STATE/PROV.	ZIP/POSTAL CODE

2 free books plus a free gift   1 free book

2 free books   Try Again!

Offer limited to one per household and not valid to current
Harlequin Superromance® subscribers. All orders subject to approval.

Visit us online at
www.eHarlequin.com

new brand-name sneakers and boots. Jake had spared no expense. The boots were lined for warmth, and the lining was removable for ease of drying.

"I've never really been up close and personal to winter clothes," said Abby. "Real winter clothes for a real long winter." She turned to Stacey. "How about trying on the new snowsuit for me. I'd love to see it."

"Okay," said Stacey as she ran upstairs. Abby flashed a look at Jake. "Doesn't seem to mind the snowsuit now."

"It's been a good evening so far," he said, happiness in his voice. "What a difference from this morning."

He was as gorgeous as his daughter. Blue eyes twinkling under thick dark lashes, head thrown back, relaxed, confident. She hadn't seen this side of him very much here in Sturbridge, but she'd bet that confidence was one of his biggest assets at the hospital. Amazing how a child could overturn an adult's world.

"Enjoy the moment," she said philosophically.

Jake raised an eyebrow, then burst into song once more as Stacey reentered the room attired in her new snowsuit.

"Beautiful," exclaimed Abby.

"Perfect," said Susan.

"Oh, Stacey," continued Abby. "You look terrific in that. The colors, the pattern. Your whole face is bright and light. Let me see how the pants are done.''

Stacey walked toward her and unzipped the pink jacket. Bib-style purple overalls with pink appliqué flowers on the legs were underneath.

''Very clever, very nice,'' said Abby.

''But I still don't want to go to school on Wednesday.'' Although her words were directed to the room in general, Stacey looked at Abby.

Abby truly hoped Jake had enjoyed his moment because it was now over. She glanced at him, but he said nothing, a sadness in his eyes. Then, from her seat on the couch, Abby reached for Stacey's hands. The girl gazed at her with curiosity.

''I know, Stacey. I know you don't want to go to school,'' Abby confirmed. ''I know you're frightened.''

Tears instantly sprang into Stacey's eyes, and Abby's heart dropped. Was she going too fast? Would Jake interfere?

''So, let's play a little game. Your cousins can play, too.'' That last was an inspired suggestion, as she saw Stacey's tears dissipate. Her mind raced thinking of the ''game'' they'd play. Something that could chip away, just chip away at the mountain in front of Stacey.

''First, we need a pretend magic wand,'' said Abby.

''We got a *real* magic wand in our room,'' answered the boys. They both raced up the stairs and were back before Abby could catch her breath, holding a long, silver, laser sword.

"This is good, right?" asked Jon, looking at Stacey.

The girl thought a minute, then nodded. "It'll do."

Abby glanced around the room, almost startled to see the rest of the family. They sat quietly, just watching. Jake leaned forward in his seat, eyes glued to Abby and Stacey. He didn't smile. He didn't nod. But he didn't stop her.

"Okay, then," began Abby. "Come on over, Jon." She stood up and positioned the boy in front of her so that he was facing the group. He held the wand in one hand while Abby placed her hand over his. "Now, close your eyes, Jon, and I'm going to ask you a question. Then we're going to pretend that this wand can grant you any wish you want."

"Okay."

"Now, this first question is for practice."

Jon nodded.

"When you get bigger, do you want to be a great baseball player or a great basketball player?"

"Ooh. This is a hard one!" He opened his eyes, searching for his brother. "Mac, what do you want to be?"

"No, no," said Abby. "No fair. This is *your* wish."

Jon shut his eyes again. "I'm going to play for the Boston Celtics. Basketball."

"All right!" said Abby. "Ready for the next one?"

"Sure."

"Remember, this is your wish. What would make you very, very happy about going to school this year?"

This time there was no hesitation. "If Mac and I are in the same class, but we don't know if we are yet."

"That's my wish, too," said Mac, piping up from his place next to his mother. "We were together in kindergarten, but everybody said, 'poor teacher.' She wasn't poor. Why'd they say that?"

Abby giggled, then turned to Stacey as everyone else laughed. "Are those cousins of yours like this all the time?"

"Yup. That's why I have to be the boss. They drive everybody crazy."

Abby took the sword and placed it in Stacey's hand. "Ready for your turn?"

"It's going to be a question about school, isn't it?"

"It's going to be a wish about school, and that's different."

"Oh. That's right. Okay." And without more prompting, Stacey closed her eyes.

"Here's your wish, Stacey," began Abby. "If

you could change just one thing about school, just one little thing, what would it be?''

Stacey's eyes squeezed shut. Abby could almost hear her thoughts, could almost smell them. Almost.

But then Stacey's eyes opened wide. She turned and glared at Abby. ''No,'' she said. ''No, no, no. I'm not playing this game. It's just like the ones they wanted me to play.'' She looked at Jake. ''You know, those *therapists*,'' she sneered. ''Those, those talking doctors.''

Stacey's abrupt anger and derision startled Abby, but she remained calm, ready to continue listening to the child.

''So, Abby,'' said Stacey, hands on hips, ''are you one of *them?*''

Abby's heart raced while she constructed a truthful answer. ''Yes, but I'm picking apples now,'' she replied quietly. ''You know that. Remember my sabbatical and my charley horse?'' Stacey nodded.

''Want to know why I'm on this vacation?'' Abby leaned forward and took Stacey's hands.

The girl nodded.

''Something very, very bad happened to me in California,'' she began in a low tone. She had the girl's full attention now. Stacey's chest barely moved as she breathed.

Abby continued. ''It was something so bad, I couldn't sleep anymore. And I had nightmares.''

"Nightmares?" asked Stacey in a whisper. "Really?"

Abby nodded.

"Bad ones?"

Abby nodded again. "Yes."

"Just like me." The child's soft voice penetrated the silent room. Then she leaned into Abby. "Can you make them stop?"

Abby laid her hand on Stacey's cheek. "I'm trying to, Stacey. I work very hard during the day so I'll be tired at night and sleep. It works most of the time."

"But I have to go to stupid school!"

"Shh, Stacey. Listen." Abby paused until Stacey's attention was on her once again. "Know what else I do?"

Stacey shook her head.

"Two more things help me. First, I tell my nightmares to a friend. When I talk about them during the day, I'm not so afraid. The dreams don't seem as scary. Have you ever told anyone about your bad dreams?"

The girl didn't answer. Then shook her head again.

Abby wanted to cry at the child's obvious pain. "Tell you what, sweetheart. I have an idea."

"What idea?"

"*If* you ever decide you want to share your dreams with a friend...and *if* you're comfortable with it, come find me. I can keep very big secrets. I'm good at that."

Stacey nodded slowly. "But I don't have to?"

"No," agreed Abby. "Only if you want to. Hey, I'm on sabbatical—no regular hours. No regular patients."

Stacey laughed.

Abby took a deep breath and exhaled. "Want to hear about the second thing I do?"

"Yes," replied Stacey without hesitation.

"I'm meeting new people and getting to know them, people like you and your family. New people, new places give me new thoughts to put into my head. I bet you could meet new people in school."

"But I don't know how," Stacey wailed. "I don't know what to say." She stamped her foot. "I hate recess and lunch periods!"

"Don't worry, Stace," came Jake's voice. "I'll call the school on Wednesday and make sure the teacher organizes some games at recess and introduces you to anyone you don't know." He turned toward Abby. "Stace has only been at the school for two years."

His daughter looked horrified and shook her head from side to side. Abby squeezed her little hand.

"Listen to me, Stace. We won't let him call the school. Don't worry. He's not going to do it."

"But, but..."

"Trust me. He won't."

Stacey glanced at her dad, who was still making noises.

"He won't? Why not?" the child asked.

"Because your daddy calling the school won't solve the problem for you."

Stacey stepped closer and put her arms around Abby. "Nobody can solve my problems. I've tried so hard." She stepped back a bit and began to rub her tummy.

"Sweetheart," said Abby, lifting Stacey to her lap, "you can solve recess and lunch all by yourself. But it takes courage."

Stacey looked at Abby with suspicious eyes, then asked, "What do I have to do?"

"Make one friend. Just one friend. Bring a jump rope to school and say, 'My name is Stacey. Want to play rope with me?'" Abby tucked her arms around Stacey as she spoke, then hugged her gently, hoping to give the child the reassurance she needed. "Think you can do that?"

"I think I can, but I don't know if I'm allowed to have friends."

Jake's voice chimed in. "What are you talking about, Pumpkin? Of course you're allowed to have friends. As many as you want."

Now Stacey's eyes filled and ran over. "You don't understand, Daddy. And I can't tell."

She jumped from Abby's lap and ran from the room, Jake in pursuit.

Abby, too, stood up and stepped forward, then paused and watched their retreat. Had she pushed too hard? Should she follow them? Her own patients didn't run out of the office; they used up every minute of their sessions. Stacey, however, wasn't her patient. No one had asked her to intervene. What in the world was she doing playing psychologist with the child?

Stop right there. She wasn't playing. For God's sake, she *was* a psychologist!

"Abby, for whatever it's worth, I thought you were wonderful," said Elinor, coming over to stand with her. "Sharing your story was above and beyond... That's the most Stacey's confided in a long, long time."

Nice hearing affirmation. "But I don't think Jake's too happy right now."

"Once he thinks about it, he will be," replied Elinor. "He wants...no, he *yearns*...for Stacey to be happy again. She's hiding something, isn't she?"

"No question about it. She thinks it's something huge and horrible," said Abby.

"And unless she confesses it..."

"It's going to keep eating at her, and those nightmares will become part of her life." There was no question about that either. Not in Abby's mind. The only question in her mind right then was Jake's reaction to the last few minutes. If he trusted her... Damn! She wished she had Stacey's counseling notes. Maybe she'd find a clue or at least a thread to unravel. She started pacing. Four other therapists had tried. Why had they failed? Why did she think she could succeed?

She had an advantage. She had access to Stacey seven days a week, twenty-four hours a day if needed.

Abby turned to Elinor. "Tell Jake I'll be at the cottage. If he wants company walking Betsy tonight, or if he wants to tell me once again to mind my own business, he'll know where to find me."

"I surely will tell him," Elinor replied. "And if he dares tell you to butt out, I'll send *him* to an analyst!"

"I OWE YOU AN APOLOGY."

Jake's greeting when she answered the knock on her door left Abby openmouthed and silent. Words of contrition were the last thing she expected. She motioned Jake and the collie inside.

"My daughter thought you were awesome," Jake continued. "Your admission to having nightmares impressed her. She'd never heard of adults having them, and I never thought to tell her."

His eyes squeezed almost shut and she saw the remorse.

"And now you feel guilty because maybe you could have eased her mind sooner." She led him to the love seats in the living room.

He nodded, with a rueful smile on his face. "But I'm not stupid or willfully blind. I made a mistake about you, Abby, and I'm sorry. You went beyond the call of duty with Stacey and actually made some headway. You were good in there, very, very good."

A warmth filled her, but she waved away the compliment. "It was only a beginning, Jake, not a happy ending or even an acceptable one."

"I couldn't agree with you more." Jake stood up and paced, then sat across from her again. "But you did make that beginning with her and I'm asking you, Abby, if you would consider working with Stacey."

The ticking of the wall clock resonated in the silent room. Abby's fingers tingled as Jake's tension vibrated through the air. His taut face said it all.

"I don't know," she began. "I don't know if I can work with Stacey...but not because I wouldn't want to. It's just that..." She wrung her hands and avoided his eyes. Jake sat still, waiting, and not saying a word.

"It's just...I don't know if I'm ready to take on a real case. The outdoor work is helping, but I'm still afraid of my own flashbacks. I still think about Officer Conroy. He's always in the back of my mind. How can I help Stacey when I haven't completed my own healing yet?"

Now she dared to look at him, wondering what he could possibly say to overcome her fears. She knew he wouldn't lie. Stacey was too important for glib answers.

He reached for her hand. "The answer's easy, Abby," he said softly. "And the answer's looking right at you."

Abby waited, eyes glued to the man.

"I'll help you," he finally said. "I'll come running day or night, whenever you need me or even if you don't. I won't let you down. You can take the lead with Stacey, but you won't be alone. And we'll figure this all out together."

Together. He meant it. She could see it in his blue eyes, now dark and warm enough to ignite her. She could hear it in his voice, low and intense. He was used to responsibility. If he said something, he'd follow through. Abby knew that much about him. His word was golden.

"I believe you," she whispered.

"Thank you," he said in the same low tone. "And I don't expect miracles, Abby. Only a little hope."

Abby laughed. "Come on, Jake. Every parent wants a miracle. Every patient wants one. We've discussed it. But miracles take hard work and I don't have Stacey's history or her agreement to spend time with me. And I don't know why four therapists gave up." She stood and put distance between them. "Will you tell me the truth?"

"They didn't give up," he said, immediately

walking toward her. "We did." He reached for her hand. "I'll tell you anything you want to know, but let's take the dog for her outing while we talk." He glanced toward Betsy, who sat at attention at the door, tail sweeping the floor as she waited to be let loose.

Abby looked at the dog and grabbed her sweater. "Let's go."

JAKE CLASPED her hand as soon as they were on the porch. "Watch your step." He pointed his flashlight ahead of them and Abby noticed how dark a moonless night could be in the country.

Betsy ran toward their road, but Jake whistled her back. "She might not be seen by a driver."

Abby shivered at the thought of anything happening to Betsy. Stacey's world would explode again. Exasperated with her thoughts, she reined in her imagination.

It was much more pleasant to think about her hand still in Jake's as they strolled together. She risked a glance at him. His head was thrown back, a small smile played on his face. He was an honorable man with a warm heart. Sexy, to boot. If circumstances were different, maybe...

Jake's fingers pressed hers, bringing her out of her reverie. She heard him sigh. "You are a real sweetheart, Abby. And beautiful, too. Do you know that?"

Startled, she attempted to pull away. "I said I'd try to help her, Jake. You don't need to roll out the compliments."

He gently grasped her shoulder and turned her to face him. His hand stroked her cheek. "It wasn't a bribe, Abby. Don't you ever look in the mirror? Your skin's so silky, your lips so full, and your voice is the sexiest thing I've ever heard."

Her heart skipped a beat. He'd caught her off guard with his words and with his sincerity. But still, a distrusting voice inside urged her on. "What, nothing about my hair and eyes? Just like your wife's, I've been told."

She was horrified as soon as the words left her mouth, but he barely flinched, just narrowed his gaze and studied her again. "You've been told wrong. You're nothing like her at all. Millions of women have brown hair and brown eyes, even *big gorgeous* brown eyes. But you're very different from Claire. How you walk, how you talk, how you view your career, how you work through your problems." He shook his head. "No, you're very different women, except maybe...underneath, where it counts." He tapped his chest. "Two good hearts."

His smile reached his eyes and ignited a warmth inside her she hadn't felt with any man in years.

"I'm sorry, Jake," she said.

"For what?"

"I shouldn't have mentioned Claire." She had to

be honest with herself and with him. "Your wife is not my business."

"Sure she is," he replied. "If you're going to work with Stacey, she is. And if you're going to take long walks with me, and I hope you are, she is. Don't apologize."

The man was either a fool or a saint.

"It's just that…" she began.

"Abby, calm down. You've been on my mind all week, driving me nuts."

"I have? Because of Stacey?"

"For starters," he admitted. "I had to protect her—I'm her dad. I'll always try to protect her, but she's not the only reason." His voice lingered as though he had more to say, so she waited. His eyes shone with warmth in the reflected moonlight as they studied her.

He leaned down, his lips brushing hers once and then again before pressing further.

She groped for his shoulders, enjoying the sensation and then closed her eyes and tasted his kiss. Delicious. Enticing. "Oh, my," she murmured, leaning back, while she felt a shudder go through Jake.

"You can say that again." He reached for her hand and gently squeezed it. "This has been quite an evening and it's not over yet."

She nodded and he started walking, wrapping his arm around her shoulder. Now the silence was calming, and Abby's racing heart slowed down. She reached around his waist, enjoying both the feel of his muscles under her hands and the weight of his arm around her. She leaned into him and felt him adjust his stride to hers as they walked on.

"So tell me about the four therapists," Abby said.

"Let's see. Two women, two men. Saturday appointments so I could take her. She went for three months to two of them. Four months to one. And five months to the last. Everything would be fine in the beginning, but after a while, she wouldn't want to continue. She'd cry and fight, even throw up.

"One time, she hid way back in the orchards. She took Betsy with her. I was scared witless, Abby. The state road runs alongside that end of the property. In the end, I told myself she just wasn't ready to face whatever she had to face. But procrastinating's not helping either. And here we are."

"Sounds as if whenever the psychologists got close to a nerve, she sabotaged the whole exercise."

"Exactly."

"So let's do things differently. No scheduled appointments. Just let her get used to me being around. I'll try to eat dinner with her during the week when Cook provides the meals outside. And when you return next week, you'll be starting your vacation, so she should be feeling pretty happy in general."

"Sounds good to me."

"We'll see. But two weeks isn't going to do it, Jake. Not with so many secrets hidden in her heart."

He squeezed her close to him. "Secrets. That's a good way of putting it. And I'm not concerned about only having two weeks. You'll be here longer than that."

Abby stepped in front of Jake and placed both hands on his cheeks. "Look at me," she said. "And remember this. I'll do my very best, but there are no guarantees. Working with a patient is like going on a voyage of discovery, and we don't know what we'll find."

"Well, I'm curious. She knows the accident wasn't her fault. I've told her that a million times. Claire was driving, Stacey was strapped into her seat belt in the back, exactly where a child is supposed to be. She didn't interfere with her mom's handling of the car."

"Where were they going?"

"To Stacey's dancing school. Like they did every week. Except this week it snowed, and Claire lost control behind the wheel."

Abby couldn't see his face in the dark, but his voice was tight. He was still coping with his memories, too.

He was a good man, a good father. He tried hard. She hated the pain he felt, the pain Stacey felt. But for the first time since she left Los Angeles, a frisson of excitement ran through her veins. Maybe she could help them. Really help them. Maybe, by the time she left Massachusetts, Jake and Stacey would be on track to happy, normal lives.

And with Jake as her own safety net, maybe she would be on the same road, too.

CHAPTER NINE

AFTER JAKE LEFT HER at the cottage, Abby enjoyed the best night's sleep she'd had since she'd left L.A. The next morning she lay in bed, blinking at the sunlight filtering through the window shades and stretching her body with the contentment of a cat.

Abby stretched one more time before jumping out of bed to get ready for the big day. The orchard was scheduled to open to the public and remain open seven days a week until the end of the season. She glanced at the clock, then peeped through the window toward the big house. She'd lived near the Templeton family long enough to know that the three children believed in early starts.

Good. The kids were outside kicking a soccer ball. All Abby had to do now was lure Stacey to her cottage and begin her work. Picking apples would have to wait.

ON FLYING FEET, Stacey intercepted the soccer ball, then stood on one leg and tapped the ball with her opposite foot, putting enough spin on it to leave her cousins kicking air. She loved this game! It was even better when her dad and uncle played, too. And when Aunt Susan used to play, they'd had three on a side. It used to be such fun, but not anymore. At least not until the new baby arrived—whenever that would be.

Stacey bit her lip, thinking about her aunt. Everyone was worried. She could tell. But Aunt Sue just smiled and said the baby needed to grow and would be just fine. Stacey wasn't sure she cared too much about the baby, but she sure cared a lot about Aunt Sue. So she helped her as much as she could. She glanced at her cousins and wrinkled her nose. The boys also tried to help sometimes, but they were useless unless someone stood over them giving directions. And that someone was usually her!

She eyed the ball and sprinted to intercept again, then suddenly heard music, music with a hard beat. She twirled and saw Abby's arm reaching high, then down in the open window. Ooh! She was dancing again. No, not dancing. Exercising.

Stacey ran after the ball in time to the music, but Jonathan beat her to it and grinned. "Bye-bye, Stacey. It's mine." And away he flew. She ignored him and spun around, wanting to catch a glimpse of Abby, but all she saw was the long white curtains shimmying in the breeze. Too bad. Watching Abby would have been fun. But at least she could hear the music. Yeah. Step left, cross right. Grapevine step.

Abby had played the same tape last time she'd worked out. She was really good. Bet she'd be a great dancer, too.

No, don't think about that!

Stacey blinked and looked around her, surprised to find herself in the middle of a grapevine step, almost on Abby's porch. She squeezed her eyes shut and rubbed her tummy, a trick that sometimes eased the familiar pain.

"Good morning, Stacey."

Startled, she opened her eyes and said nothing. But there was Abby, standing on the porch, smiling at her. She was so friendly that every part of her smiled, not only her mouth, but also her eyes, especially in the corners. And last night, when she'd held Stacey on her lap, she smelled so good, too.

"Hi," Stacey finally replied.

"I was hoping you'd join me," said Abby.

"You were?"

"I sure was." Abby opened the door and held it wide. "It's lonely doing all these aerobics by myself. I could definitely use a partner."

Stacey would love to...just love to be Abby's partner, but...she shook her head. "Remember, Abby," Stacey whispered, "I told you I wasn't allowed to dance."

Abby motioned her inside. Then Abby lowered the music's volume and bent down until they could see into each other's eyes.

"And you need to remember," Abby said, "that *I* told *you* exercise is not dancing. Aerobics is hard work! We think about using all our muscle groups and giving our hearts and lungs a good workout so they'll remain healthy and strong. Does that sound like a dance teacher talking?"

No, no, it didn't. And suddenly Stacey heard herself giggling, something only her cousins did. She looked at Abby—the lady who had nightmares just like her, the lady who knew how to make friends, the lady who something really bad had happened to—and suddenly Stacey threw herself at Abby and held tight. "It's not dancing, is it?" she asked. "Is it?"

Abby hugged her, too, and touched noses with her, then moved her head from side to side. "Here's an Eskimo kiss that says the answer's no."

Stacey wanted to dissolve in Abby's arms. She suddenly couldn't move and wanted to stay there forever. "I'm tired," she said, and felt Abby's embrace tighten.

"Is it a good tired?"

"Uh-huh."

"I'm glad," said Abby. "It means you're relaxed now, and happy to be here."

"Yes."

"And in another minute, you'll be squirming away from me, anxious to get moving to the music."

Stacey peeped at Abby. "How about right now?"

"Sure," said Abby, standing up and pulling Stacey with her. "So, on the weekends, we'll work out in the mornings, and during the week, in the evenings. Is that a deal?"

"Yes, yes, yes."

"Then, let's do it!" Abby adjusted the volume of the tape player once more.

JAKE WALKED OUT the back door ready to join the kids' soccer game, keep them busy for a time and give his sister-in-law some well-deserved rest. Later he and Robert would put the children to work at the petting zoo where they could host young visitors to the orchard. With the early contractions and discomfort she'd been having, Susan needed as few responsibilities as possible, but her own doctor would have final say about her schedule after she saw him this week.

His eyes scanned the area, easily spotting the two identical blond heads of his nephews. "Hi, guys," he called, jogging closer toward them. "Did you kick my daughter out of the game or what?"

"Hi, Uncle Jake. Wanna play?" Two sets of blue eyes gleamed at him expectantly.

"That's what I'm here for, but where's Stacey?"

"Up there," said Jon, waving at the cottage while trying to keep the ball in play at his feet. "I got the ball away from her, and then, *poof!* she was gone."

"Yeah. *Poof!* She was gone," echoed Mac.

"Right to Abby's house. Listen, Uncle Jake. Hear the music?"

Jake paused for a moment and cocked his head. "Sure do and I'm going to investigate—but you two stay here." He could read those boys' minds as easily as he could read the morning paper. Always ready for action, they were eager to join him now. He had to sweeten the pot. "When I get back, we'll get your dad and have a short soccer game. How's that?"

"Yes!" Instantly the boys went back to kicking the ball between them, satisfied by Jake's promise.

As he walked toward Abby's cottage, Jake chuckled at the simplicity with which Jon and Mac operated most of the time. Happiness was a soccer ball. Or a bat and ball. Or blueberry picking. Of course, the boys were very young, very much loved and protected by two terrific parents. A strong beginning—just like the one he and Claire had given Stacey. Jake hoped like hell nothing ever happened to spoil it for his nephews.

The music pulsed more strongly as he approached the little house. The curtains billowed, beckoning him to peep through the screen. He didn't hesitate. If Stacey and Abby were together so soon, he'd want to see them with his own eyes and cheer.

He stood quietly to the side of the window, watching the images inside the generous living area. Instantly, his heart filled with joy at the sight of Abby and Stacey moving to the music. Two lithe bodies, graceful and sure, Stacey following Abby's every move. His daughter was grinning, totally animated. She giggled once, then giggled again. And his heart almost stopped completely as the years rolled backward.

This Stacey was the real one. *This* Stacey was the daughter he remembered. At this moment with Abby, his little girl was laughing like a regular kid! He closed his eyes and leaned against the wall, grateful for its support and thankful for the day, thankful for being given new hope.

When he opened his eyes, nothing around him had changed, and yet everything inside him had changed. Anything was possible. Anything. The dancers, however, ignorant of his discoveries, continued exercising, and Jake moved to the center of the window and watched.

Now Abby captured his attention. His eyes devoured her beautiful face and sexy, graceful body as she stretched, lunged and stepped to the music. Nothing on earth beat the combination of long, shapely legs and black spandex shorts over a cute round bottom. A bottom that would fill his hand perfectly. His breath caught; his pants tightened. He wanted to take her in his arms and make love to her. Instead, he inhaled deeply three times and wiped his mouth with the back of his hand.

He could have stood there all morning, but Stacey spotted him through the window.

"Abby said it was okay to exercise," she called while slowing her routine.

"Of course it is," Jake agreed, smiling at Stacey but catching Abby's eye.

"Come in," said Abby, waving him inside. "You'll have to wait until we finish this combination if you want to talk to Stacey." She turned to the child. "We have to keep going, Stace, so our muscles don't cool down too fast."

"I know that," Stacey replied as she picked up the pace. "We always used to have a cool-down period…" Her voice trailed off and her mouth tightened. She darted a nervous glance at Jake before concentrating again on the exercise.

She's afraid! Of what? Me? Jake's mind spun in fifty directions as he tried to make sense of one frightened glance. He almost missed Abby's remarks.

"Did you used to belong to a gym, Stacey? Is that why you're so good now?" Abby grinned as she faced the girl; they were now mirror images as they continued the routine.

"Nope," said Stacey. "I just know about muscles and stuff."

The music came to an end, but Abby motioned Stacey to continue stepping from side to side with her. "Just until your dad leaves, then we'll pick up the beat again."

STACEY WISHED her dad would go away before he said something she didn't want to hear. Something about long ago. About the time when everything was good. She risked a quick glance at him. Oh, no! He had that special look on his face as he watched her exercise. Smiles everywhere. Her dad loved her to pieces! He thought she was wonderful, but she didn't deserve it. And it made her ache. If she could just do exercises with Abby and not think about anything else, she'd be all right.

She closed her eyes and prayed. *Please, Daddy, go play soccer with the boys and leave me alone with Abby. And most of all, don't say anything about my old dancing school.* Okay, so maybe it wasn't a proper prayer, but it was exactly what she wanted now.

"You two girls are heading for Radio City Music Hall," said Jake. "I could watch all day."

Stacey groaned silently and glanced at her dad. Then looked again. For once, he wasn't focused on her. Instead, he was staring at Abby, and Abby's face turned from soft pink to rosy red. She was blushing! Stacey pivoted back toward Jake. His eyes were smiling, his mouth was smiling in that special way he used on her. But he was looking only at Abby this time!

A tingle danced down Stacey's spine. She carefully checked out the two adults again—left, right, left, right—as though she were at a tennis match. Daddy—Abby. Daddy—Abby. Her dad and Abby! Wow!

But…rocks tumbled in her stomach. What could she be thinking? She couldn't start to love Abby. Not after what happened to Mommy. Even if she liked Abby and Abby liked her. Even if she wanted to, she wasn't allowed. Oh, God. Everything was too hard. Too complicated. Step left. Step right. She concentrated on stepping side to side with Abby.

"So what do you think of my little dancer?" asked Jake as he leaned in to give Stacey a quick kiss. "Isn't she great?"

"It's not dancing! It's aerobics. Exercise," said Stacey in a big voice.

Jake shrugged. "You're moving to the music. You're a natural, sweetheart. So, maybe we could find you another dance… I mean, how about a gymnastics school here in Sturbridge? Let's ask around."

Nausea almost choked her. He meant to say dancing school. She just knew it. Stacey scrambled toward the door. She had to get out of here, to be alone where no one could see her.

A pair of gentle arms stopped her in flight. "You don't have to dance, Stacey, unless you want to." Abby's soft voice. "And your father's going to shut up about it from now on. I promise you that. And you and I will do whatever we feel like doing. Stretching, marching, climbing apple trees, feeding the baby animals, making cider…even playing soccer with the family. We'll do whatever we want to do."

She loved Abby's voice. It was so calm and quiet. So different from the nagging voice in her mind, the voice that wouldn't let her forget. She wished that voice would go away. She wished she could dance again. She wished she could go back and live that awful day over again, but this time it would be different. This time she wouldn't make her mom die.

Suddenly, tears fell. It was all too much. The past and the present. She clung to Abby even when her dad tried to pry her away. She loved him so much, but she couldn't face him. Abby understood.

"She has to work it out, Jake," Stacey heard Abby say. "If she wants those tummy aches to disappear, she has to figure out how to share her problem. How to share her pain."

Share it? She could never do that. She couldn't tell anybody. Could she?

THE ORCHARD WAS NOW OPEN for business and people swarmed everywhere. Abby stood with Maureen selling half-bushel bags to the pick-your-own-apples visitors, while Elinor worked in the gift shop, and

Stacey and the boys stayed with the small children's zoo.

"It's as though people marked today on their calendars," Abby said to Maureen. "The parking lot's almost full."

Maureen squeezed her arm with affection. "They have done just that. It's always the same. Big crowds."

Abby scanned the vicinity and saw Jake transporting customers by hay wagon into the far fields. "Jake really gets involved when he's home, doesn't he?"

"He sure does," responded Maureen. "He grew up on this land. He always takes vacation during the harvest season, not during the summer like most people. He loves to be part of the action.

"And speaking of Jake," Maureen added, "how are you getting on with him? I've always had a soft spot for that boy."

Her aunt's ploy was so obvious, Abby could barely contain her smile. "Jake is...um...okay."

"Just okay?" Maureen's voice registered disbelief. "Have you no eyes, dear? The young man's gorgeous! He's everything a woman could want."

Despite herself, Abby felt a faint heat rise to her cheeks.

"Ach. You did notice! Now I'm a happy woman."

Abby groaned silently. She'd have to remember

that her loving aunt didn't give up easily when she was on a mission.

"You've got three customers lined up," said Abby. "Let *that* make you a happy woman."

AN EVENING WALK with Jake—after the crowds and Aunt Mo were gone and dinner with the family was over—seemed the most natural activity in the world. As natural as holding hands with him. Abby didn't know exactly how their fingers wound up intertwined, but they did. He'd held the door, told her to watch her step and suddenly her hand was in his. And she had no desire to pull away.

Now she glanced from their clasped hands to his face, admiring the inherent strength she saw there. Strength of character. Determination. Responsibility. She'd seen him trip and stumble in his interaction with Stacey many times, maybe every time, but she'd never seen him give up. Not in speech, not in action, and she'd bet a month's salary, not even in thought.

A good man. Abby heard echoes of Maureen's voice. She blinked and looked away. It wasn't only his strength of character she admired. His strong jaw, firm mouth and those twinkling blue eyes spelled temptation. Add his tight buns covered by a pair of snug faded jeans and the guy had enough sex appeal to make her squirm. Her breath caught before she exhaled.

"That was a big sigh," said Jake. "What are you thinking?"

"I'm thinking that you're a very good father." *And damn appealing to a woman who isn't supposed to think about relationships until she returns home!*

His reply sounded like a snort. "Right, Abby. Everything out of my mouth is wrong. I make my daughter cry and get stomachaches, for God's sake."

"But she knows you love her unconditionally."

"So what?" he asked, frustration in his tone. "That's nothing new. She's had my love from the minute she was born, and it doesn't seem to help."

"That's where you're wrong," Abby said with conviction, halting their steps. She pulled out of his grasp and faced him, her hands gesturing as she spoke. "Your love is her anchor. *You* are her anchor in a very rough sea."

"She seems more comfortable with you."

She waved his remark aside. "I'm just safer for the moment. She's got no history with me…yet. But as I start probing, she might back away pretty quickly."

"But you won't give up, will you?" he asked, a trace of concern in his voice.

"Not as long as you don't."

"Not a chance," Jake replied. "She's stuck with me for the rest of her life. Good times, bad times.

I'll be there for her. Right now, I just wish she'd unload whatever secrets she's carrying."

Abby nodded, and impulsively squeezed his arm. "I do too. She is toting too much baggage for a little girl."

"Yeah," he sighed, reaching for her hand again. "That's why my hopes were up this morning. She was so happy with you, doing those exercises, which still look like dancing to me."

"Ah, there's that word again."

"But you should have seen her, Abby," Jake continued. "Right from the beginning in her crib, when she heard music, she boogied her whole body, waving her arms, legs, everything. The music is in her."

"I know," Abby replied. "But right now, the very word *dancing* seems to upset her. Maybe in time she'll tell us why. And then we can help her recapture the joy she used to feel."

Suddenly, he stroked her cheek, his fingers gentle as they traced her lips. "How'd you get so smart, lady?" he whispered.

His eyes captured hers; she couldn't look away, didn't want to look away. The moonlight illuminated his face as he leaned closer, and she lifted her chin toward him. Her heart beat a quick rhythm of its own. Anticipation. She'd been waiting for his touch all day.

His kiss was gentle, thoughtful, as his tongue traced the soft outline of her lips. A shiver pulsed through her entire body. Her eyes closed as she tasted where he had been. Mmm... She lifted her face for more and didn't have to wait. Jake's tongue met hers and gently explored her mouth.

She wound her arms around his neck and leaned closer. She inhaled spice and clean man, and the aroma whet her appetite. It had been a long time since anyone had kissed her like this.

She returned his kiss with an eagerness that surprised her, and all rational thought disappeared. She reveled in the moment. In Jake's arms. Reveled in Jake's kisses. And had no desire to stop.

But suddenly, the kisses did stop. She moaned in protest and slowly raised her eyelids until she looked into Jake's stunned face. "What?" she asked, her wits not yet active.

He managed a chuckle. "Yeah, I'm asking myself the same question." The laugh disappeared. "You're beautiful, Abby, you're fantastic, and I want to make love with you in the worst way...no, make that the best way. And if we keep this up, I think we will." His voice questioned, his eyebrow raised in inquiry.

He was deferring to her.

Suddenly, a cold reality replaced the heat. How could she allow herself to get involved with someone she'd never see again after she left Sturbridge? How could she get romantically involved with Stacey's father when Stacey was so vulnerable right now? When they were all so vulnerable right now? The answer was simple. She couldn't.

She offered an apologetic smile. "I'm afraid, Jake, that good sense calls for limits. We're only asking for complications. And none of us—Stacey included—needs any more complications."

Jake's mouth tightened. He nodded and said nothing.

THE NEXT MORNING, Abby sat in the kitchen of the big house and discovered a new complication. This time it involved Susan and Robert, or rather, Susan's pregnancy. The couple had made an emergency visit to the hospital in the middle of the night. Hours of regular abdominal contractions in a seven-month pregnancy qualified as a serious situation in everyone's mind, including the obstetrician's, and his directives were clear and concise after his examination.

"Total bed rest," Robert repeated to the assembled family, his complexion as pale as the milk in his sons' plastic cups. He lifted Susan's hand to his mouth and kissed her palm. "No activity for this lady, none of any kind except walking to the bathroom. The contractions have stopped for now, but if they start again, I'll be taking her back to the hospital and leaving her there."

Abby watched Susan stroke her stomach, her hand curved in a protective arch, her mouth tight, her chin stubborn. Tears stung Abby's eyes as she recognized the primordial instinct.

Susan suddenly focused her attention on Abby. "I need you, Abby," she said. "*We* need you. The children have to get off to school every day, their lunches have to be made, and next weekend will be even busier than this one. Thank God Jake is still here today because it's Labor Day, but from now on the crowds will get bigger…"

"Shush, Susie Q," said Robert, kissing his wife's head. "We'll handle it."

"How, without extra help?" she retorted.

Silence descended for a moment. "Susan's right," said Elinor slowly as she turned toward Abby. "The weekend crowds will get bigger for the next six weeks. Robert and I have a business to run and three children to watch. Jake is going back to Boston in the morning. I just can't do it all."

"But I don't know anything about the business," said Abby. "I don't see how I could help very much."

"I do," said Elinor, taking Abby's hand. "If you would consider switching jobs and becoming our chief-cook-and-bottle-washer for a while—a sort of combination nanny-housekeeper—you would be helping immeasurably. The children already like you so much. Susan could relax knowing a capable person was in charge of her troop, and so could I."

When Abby didn't respond, Elinor continued.

"Of course, you'd still have the cottage and your privacy, and we'd pay you more than you're earning in the orchards...."

Abby waved her hand at the mention of money, but a yellow caution light blinked in her mind. Closer contact with the family. Intimate contact with Stacey and Jake. If she agreed, she'd be with both father and daughter several times during the day once Jake's vacation began. Family activities built relationships. And she'd be smack in the center of it all.

Abby looked around the kitchen. Everyone's eyes but Jake's were on her, and she felt a collective breath being held. Jake seemed to be watching some distant scene beyond the window.

What was he thinking? Did he want her to say no? Is that why he wouldn't meet her eyes? That didn't make sense, not after their recent conversations and other...encounters. No, he didn't want her to say no. Not really. But maybe there was a vestige of fear still lurking. Yes, he wanted Abby on his team, working with Stacey, but he also wanted to set the pace and keep control. She couldn't promise that. Not when dealing with volatile emotions and hidden fears.

She smiled at Elinor. "Sure, I'll be happy to do what I can," she replied, glancing again at Jake to gauge his reaction. And there it was. A half grin and a millimeter of relief in his expression. Had he been afraid she wouldn't step in and help?

"Think you can handle this family?" Jake asked nonchalantly as he walked toward her.

"I come from a family of cops," she said, looking around the room. "Two big brothers, uncles and cousins. A terrific mom and a high-ranking dad who has his own ideas about how to protect everyone." An image of her dad standing with her in her office flashed through her mind. "It makes for interesting conversation," she continued as she grinned at the boys. "I was the only girl child and I handled them all." She leaned closer to the twins and whispered. "I can handle you!"

The twins giggled as she'd wanted them to, and even Stacey laughed.

"You were the only girl, just like me?" she asked.

"Sure was. Still am. I have three nephews and no nieces." She looked at Stacey. "So that makes us pretty special."

Stacey grinned. "Yup."

"No argument here," said Jake as he gave his daughter a kiss on the cheek and then sauntered to Abby.

No! She felt her face heat at the thought of him kissing her in front of everyone.

Elinor saved the moment. "So, we're all agreed. Abby, you're in charge!"

CHAPTER TEN

"I DON'T KNOW WHERE the day went...oh, excuse me." Abby yawned as she shrugged into her sweater, ready to take a walk with Jake and Betsy that evening. The children were asleep, the kitchen cleaned up and the other adults had retired for the night.

"Maybe being the house-boss is too much work," said Jake with a frown as he followed her through the back door. "You wanted outside work in the fresh air where you could exhaust yourself and sleep soundly at night."

Abby yawned again. "In case you haven't noticed," she said, patting him on the arm, "I *am* exhausted. I will sleep tonight, and in case you hadn't realized, Aunt Mo and I were outside for part of the day."

"That's right," said Jake. "I saw you. No customer walked away with less than two bags each."

"You can thank Aunt Mo for that," said Abby with a grin. "The lady can sell. She knew half the folks who came today. And between customers, she regaled me with songs from her show…if I hear 'Hello, Dolly!' one more time…'' She laughed and felt Jake's arms come around her.

"I love that happy sound—sexy, too! And I've noticed it more and more these last few days."

She leaned into him, held him close. "I know," she whispered. "I'm more relaxed than when I arrived. I hope it's a sign that the flashbacks are in the past and my emotional strength is returning."

His arms tightened around her. "I know you'll give your practice a hundred and ten percent whenever you decide to return to work."

"Well," she replied, "my patients always get everything I can give, but…you know, last time 'everything' wasn't enough."

He didn't reply immediately, and Abby tried not to let the silence feel too painful. Then Jake turned, took her hand and led her along their familiar route. "The only thing I know for sure," he finally said in a calm voice, "is that you have to move forward."

He was right. But wasn't moving forward what she'd been trying to do? A month had passed since Officer Conroy's death, and in Abby's mind she'd been making progress. When she'd telephoned Martin Bernstein last time, she'd detected only approval and reassurance. Maybe she was stronger than she thought.

But was she ready for a full caseload of patients?

A tremor ran through her, and she had her answer. For now, she'd stick to helping one little girl.

HE FELT THE QUIVER travel down her body. "Cold?" he asked, simultaneously tucking her under his arm. She leaned into him again, and his heart smiled before his mouth did.

"Warm enough now?" He breathed the words into her hair and inhaled a hint of floral with a touch of...peach? Delicious. As delicious as Abby herself.

He wanted her, no doubt about it. A wonderful surprise. He hadn't thought there would be another woman in his life for a very long time. Not with all the unresolved emotional ties that were part of his life. Stacey certainly was the biggest part. But there was more. Jake, too, had his memories and guilts. Claire hadn't deserved her fate. She'd been a sweet woman, a wonderful mother and a loyal wife. She shouldn't have driven that day!

He closed his eyes for a moment and took a deep breath, once again focusing his thoughts on Abby. A quiet peace filled him and he smiled. "You smell so good."

"That's eau de baby powder," she joked. "The twins are brutal in the bath and beyond. It was like a snowstorm in there. I won't turn my back next time."

"Ah, sweetheart, I think we've thrown too much at you. Rob can handle the boys tomorrow."

He felt her stillness then. Felt her slip from his embrace. Felt her cool hands lightly pressing his cheeks. She captured him with her big eyes and he couldn't look away.

"That's twice, Jake," she said.

"Twice?"

"And I don't take it lightly. Not from you."

"Take what lightly?"

"You, ah…called me…sweetheart. Twice now. I don't think you really want to use that word. It could upset someone around here."

She meant Stacey, of course. And she had a point, particularly since he hadn't realized he'd used the endearment so freely. But when he looked at Abby's lovely face, he wanted to hold her in his arms and call her sweetheart all night.

"Do you think it's possible," he asked as he pulled her gently to his chest, "for us to live our lives one day at a time? For two adults to allow their relationship to evolve naturally? Normally?"

A worry line marred her forehead, but she squeezed his arm. "But our situation isn't normal, is it Jake?"

He couldn't lie to Abby and he couldn't lie to himself. Their situation was not normal and perhaps it never would be.

ON FRIDAY EVENING, Abby procrastinated in the kitchen while keeping an ear tuned to Jake's arrival from Boston. He had called her every night that week. Of course, he spoke with Stacey first, and then called back after Abby had returned to the cottage. Earlier in the week, on the evening before school started, Abby couldn't decide who was more nervous—father or daughter. Truth was, she also felt on edge, but did her best to hide it.

And on the first day of school, she'd prepared lunches, driven all three children to the bus stop at the end of their long road and hugged them before they boarded.

"Just smile and say hi," she whispered to Stacey. "You'll make a friend or two."

"It doesn't matter," Stacey replied, her voice flat, her face devoid of expression.

"I'll be waiting for you," said Abby, giving the girl an extra hug. Her heart went out to the child who was trying so hard to be brave.

At three o'clock, the kids had clattered down the bus's steps and into her waiting car. Stacey had the front seat.

"The work's easy," she offered.

Not what Abby had worried about at all. "That's great, I guess," said Abby, "but if you're bored, we can always come up with some more challenging extra homework."

A wrinkled nose was the only reply. The twins clamored for attention then and further opportunity with Stacey was lost.

Jake hadn't had any better luck, Abby discovered that evening when she spoke with him on the phone. And then they spoke of other things—his work, her busy day, Susan's condition, an item in the paper. She loved the sound of his voice. She loved their conversations. And she looked forward to the weekend when Jake would begin his two-week vacation.

And he'd be arriving any minute now. Stacey was waiting on the front porch as usual, Betsy at her side. Abby stayed away, wanting to give Stacey all the privacy possible, hoping that when she and Jake were together in person, the child would share her week with him. Not that she and Stacey weren't spending time together. Every night, Stacey came to her ready for their exercise routines. Sadly, thought Abby, it seemed to be the highlight of the child's day.

"Daddy's coming," called Stacey through the front door, her voice excited for the first time all week.

Abby couldn't help smiling as she heard the hum of the car's engine, but she consciously planted her feet on the kitchen floor. Stacey and Jake could have their privacy now. She and Jake would have time together later.

THE FIRST WEEKEND of Jake's vacation sped by with more visitors to the orchards than Abby thought possible. Harvesttime was an intense eight weeks with several different activities going on simultaneously. Excitement and stress mingled with satisfaction among the family members, and Jake thrived in the midst of it all. Now Abby really understood his devotion to the farm. He worked as hard as Robert; together with their mother, they ran a strong business.

Abby knew that Rob was particularly glad to have Jake home because of Susan. The poor guy made regular checks on his wife by cell phone or in person during the day, despite the fact that either Abby or, on the weekend, Aunt Mo, was no farther than the next room most of the time.

Stacey was also putting her heart into the weekend work. Attacking her assignments at the orchard, Stacey was in her element. Everything she needed was right here. Two weeks with a full-time dad could seem like a long time to a child, long enough for Stacey to feel happy.

THE BACK DOOR SLAMMED and footsteps clattered across the kitchen floor after school on Monday, the fourth day of the school year. "I have a new friend," called Stacey.

Abby left Susan lying on the sofa in the living room and went to meet the troops. While the weather was good, the children walked home from the bus stop together.

"A new friend? That's wonderful," Abby said,

giving Stacey a special smile. The girl's grin broadened. Her eyes shone.

"Where's Mommy?" asked Jon as he asked every time he bounced into the house.

Abby nodded toward the "Susan" room, which was slowly reflecting its occupant's activities with books, jigsaw puzzles, crossword puzzles and needlework projects spread across the low table next to the couch. "Gently, boys," Abby admonished. "Remember, soft kisses, no climbing."

"We know. We know," said Mac as he trotted down the hall, Jon in pursuit.

Abby held out her hand to Stacey. "Come on. I've got to watch them, but you can tell me about your new friend as I do my guard duty."

Stacey giggled. "The boys like you, Abby. They really do. They just don't like Aunt Susan being...you know...on the couch all the time. And I don't like it either."

In a heartbeat, the child's giggles turned into deep, quavering inhalations. Her lips trembled in an effort not to cry.

"Let's visit your aunt," said Abby, reaching for Stacey's hand, "and you'll see how well she is. Resting is making her happier." It was the truth, Abby thought as she and Stacey went into the living room together. Every day without contractions made Susan less anxious.

The mother-to-be was propped up against a slew

of pillows and was holding up something for her boys to see. Jon and Mac sat on two chairs adjacent to the couch—the chairs they'd been assigned to use. Abby laughed as she recalled Stacey's comments of a few days ago. "We can train the boys like we trained Betsy," she'd whispered as she watched her uncle go over the rules for visiting Susan.

Now Abby leaned down to Stacey. "I think the training worked, don't you?"

"Yes," Stacey said with a big grin. And Abby breathed a sigh of relief.

"Hi, ladies," said Susan. "Come see what I'm showing the boys."

Abby and Stacey stood behind Jon and Mac.

"I've started to knit a sweater for each of my sons, and when the sweaters are finished, it will be time for the baby to be born."

"Yeah! So can you knit real fast, Mom?" asked Jon.

"That's right," echoed Mac. "The faster you knit, the faster the baby comes and then you can get out of bed and everything will be okay."

Abby shook her head and hid her grin behind her hand, but saw Susan's eyes fill with tears.

"They don't get it," said Stacey with hands on her hips. She threw a kiss at her aunt. "Don't cry, Aunt Sue. I'll straighten them out." She glared at her cousins. "Will you two use your brains for a minute?"

The boys were mute. Abby watched, as Stacey held sway.

"The sweaters are going to grow just a little bit each day to match how the baby grows. When the sweaters are done, the baby will be done." She paused, exasperated. "So, knitting faster won't help. Now do you understand?"

The boys nodded, and Stacey turned to Abby. "Do you see why I have to be the boss around here?" She spoke from her heart, her face as serious as could be.

"But they're only six years old," said Abby, biting her lip to contain her laughter.

Then Stacey paused. Her eyelids closed and she leaned against Abby. "Six years old," she ruminated. "I remember being six." She smiled dreamily. "We had fun. Mommy walked me to school every day. And back, too. And on Saturdays, we went to the zoo. Or the special museum for kids where you can touch everything. Or we made brownies and cookies, and Daddy said he'd get too fat, but he ate them all anyway."

Her deep sigh filled the air and she leaned more heavily against Abby. Abby held her close, kissed her cheek, then glanced at Susan. The other woman looked stunned.

"Six," Stacey continued in a low voice, "six was good. I liked it. I wish I could still be..." Her eyes snapped open then. "But it doesn't work like that, does it?'' she asked Abby, anger lacing her voice. ''I can't be six again. I can't go back, can I?''

Abby kneeled on the floor, at eye level with Stacey. She squeezed the child's hands. ''No, my love. You can't. But we can do the opposite. We can go forward. And if you want me to be with you, we'll go forward together. You won't be alone. And neither will I.''

Stacey didn't stir for a moment, then almost toppled Abby to the ground with her exuberant hugs. Abby's arms wrapped around Jake's child.

''You're different from the others, Abby,'' said Stacey. ''I like you. A lot. I really do.''

Abby's tears flowed unchecked.

JAKE GLANCED at his watch as he chatted with some of the workers who'd gathered before dinner. The kids would have long since returned home from school, but he hadn't spotted Stacey yet today. He clapped one of the foremen on the shoulder, thanked him for his good work and headed into the house. His thoughts fluctuated between the orchard and his family.

The harvest had gotten off to a strong start. Templeton Orchards had a full complement of seasonal employees, and the weather forecast couldn't be better. The crop of Macs and Courtlands exceeded expectations. The Empires would peak in a week or so, then the Red Delicious and Golden Delicious...

He opened the back door, walked the few steps into the kitchen and came to a standstill. Something felt different. He examined the room. The furnishings all appeared to be in place. He looked at his daughter sitting at the table doing her homework. He glanced at Abby sitting next to her. The atmosphere was peaceful. Calm.

"Hi, Daddy," said Stacey, lifting her head and focusing on him, a smile illuminating her face.

Her expression hit him with the force of a lightning bolt. Her smile belonged to the old Stacey. He took slow careful breaths, afraid to jump to conclusions, afraid to hope too much. The change he'd noticed when he walked into the room came not from furniture rearrangement but from his daughter and…he shifted his gaze to Abby. She winked and nodded imperceptibly toward the girl. He studied his child again. She was…relaxed! A tiny smile played on her face. The pain in her eyes was gone.

His heart started to pound. Something big had happened while he was out in the fields.

"Hi, baby," he said, bending down to give Stacey a kiss. "How was school?"

"Good," Stacey replied. "The homework's easy and I have a new friend. Her name is Cynthia and I invited her over after school on Friday. Her mom's going to write a note so she can go on my bus. Is that okay?"

Okay? Hallelujah! She could have ten friends visiting if she wanted to. "It's fine with me. But you have to ask Abby, since she's the one in charge around here."

"Oh, Abby already said yes."

He glanced at Abby.

"No problem here," she assured him.

"Are you sure you're not a magician?" he murmured, leaning over her chair and nuzzling her nape. "Stacey's made a friend after all this time. I can hardly believe it."

"No supernatural powers," Abby replied, one hand raised to stroke his mouth as she continued talking. "Just right place, right time. And there's more, but I advise caution before you get too excited." She reclined in her chair, putting her delicious neck out of reach, and cocked her head toward him. "Let's just say, it's been an interesting day and I'll fill you in later."

He could wait to hear the details, but he wished he could kiss the breath from her now. His arms ached to hold her; his heart yearned to touch hers.

"What?" she asked. "What are you staring at?"

"You," he finally said with a chuckle. "Just you."

She blushed, and he chuckled again. Damn, he was glad she had another two months with them. A lot could happen in two months, and he'd do everything in his power to make sure it did.

FATIGUE HIT ABBY that night. "Either I'm not as fit as I thought, or housework and child care really do knock a person out," she joked as she and Jake cut their walk short and headed back toward the cottage. "But I don't want to disappoint Betsy. At least throw her another stick so she'll get some extra exercise."

Jake complied, then wrapped his arm around her. "I'm going to hire a cleaning service. There's too much work between the kids, the house, Susan and your dealing with customers. No wonder you're tired."

Abby knew her weariness was due to more than physical activity. Emotionally, she'd had an exhausting day. She'd explained Jake's daughter's visit to her six-year-old self, explained her reactions to the notion of moving forward together. But she'd omitted the hugs and the "I like you" part. Too sticky.

In the two months ahead, Abby hoped Stacey would gain perspective on their relationship, and that when Abby's visit came to an end, Stacey would be able to take it in stride with the promise of phone calls and e-mails.

"A cleaning service isn't necessary," Abby protested. "There's time to straighten up when the kids are in school. I'm just not used to the schedule yet."

"I'm calling tomorrow," he insisted. "It's a big house and every adult here works the business. No one has time to clean bathrooms. End of subject."

The steamroller approach. Something new. "Your brother or mother might have something to say about it. Cleaning services are expensive."

"My contribution. They won't say a word."

Then again, sometimes steamrolling got things done. Abby shrugged. She *was* tired.

Jake escorted her up the two steps of the lighted porch and opened the front door of the cottage.

"I'm sorry for being a par—ty poo—per," she said, trying unsuccessfully to hide her yawn behind her hand.

"As long as it's not due to the company you keep in the evenings," he replied with a woeful expression. "Boring a woman to sleep is not exactly a boost to my ego."

Boring! Not quite. The give-and-take she and Jake had shared during their walks together were anything but. Work, patients, books, movies, politics, philosophies, Boston, Los Angeles. The list of topics went on. If she spent fifty years in conversation with him, they'd always find new ideas to explore.

She managed to grin at him. "You are many things, Jake, but boring isn't one of them."

"What a relief!" He swiped his forehead with exaggerated gestures. "Now I can proceed with this." And he lowered his head until his lips pressed against hers.

Immediately, her heartbeat went into overdrive. How did he manage to do that to her every time?

Spontaneous combustion, a unique experience for her.

She kissed him back with everything she had. Despite her fatigue. Despite the busy day. There was just something about this man...

"Oh, sweetheart," murmured Jake a while later, "life is never boring with you, either."

She ducked her head and scooted into the house, now wondering how she'd ever fall asleep.

JAKE WHISTLED for Betsy as he left the cottage porch. He'd give the dog a treat—another romp down the road. He shook his head. His decision wasn't based on Betsy's needs, but his own. There was no way he could turn in now. Not after that sizzle with Abby.

Jake picked up speed and Betsy barked excitedly. They passed the business office, the cider house and the store. Lights were still on in the bunkhouses, and Jake waved to a few people who stood outside chatting. After running half a mile, he slowed to a jog and continued until he reached the end of the property line, just bordering the state highway. He loped around and started the jog back.

No matter how hard he ran, he couldn't stop thinking of Abby. He suspected he'd be running laps back to the state road several more times before his libido could be quashed. Either laps or a cold shower. That woman was fire in his blood! And if her kisses were any indication, he'd bet his last diagnostic catheter that the feeling was mutual.

"Come on, Betsy," he invited as he started his second outbound lap. "We'll both sleep well tonight." Twenty minutes later the darkened cottage came into view, and Jake reversed directions, ready for a third mile.

But Betsy stood her ground facing the cottage. She lifted her snout in the air and whined. Jake came to a halt. "What, girl? What is it?"

The dog ran toward the small house, then looked back at Jake.

"Abby's not coming on this run, Bets. She's sound asleep. Come on." Jake started back down the road, confident Betsy would follow, and almost tripped on the dog as she circled in front of him. Soft barks and another trot toward the cottage had Jake following her this time.

"What's the matter, girl?"

"Yip, yip, yip." The dog made a beeline for the front door and whined.

"Shh. Abby's sleeping," whispered Jake.

Betsy ran off the porch, turned to look at him and raced to the side of the house. He followed, stopping only when the dog did. Right beneath Abby's bedroom window. The dog looked up at him, and Jake stood completely still.

And then he heard the sobs—deep heartwrenching sobs—interspersed with words he couldn't distinguish. He ran back to the porch and turned the doorknob. No luck. The city girl had locked the door. He dug into his pocket and found a set of master keys. An eternity passed before he located the correct one. And then he was inside, almost tripping in the dark in his haste to get to Abby's room.

He snapped on the night-table lamp and sat at the edge of her bed, for a moment undecided how to bring her out of her nightmare. Beads of perspiration dotted her forehead; her eyes were closed, but tears streaked down her cheeks.

"Ohmygod! Ohmygod. So much blood." Her head rocked back and forth like an out-of-control metronome. And her voice, her beautiful sexy voice, now strained on one note, high-pitched and scared.

A chill ran through him. She was back where this journey had started. His heart ached for her, and he took her cold hand and started rubbing it. "Abby," he called in a soft voice. "Time to wake up. Come on. It's over."

"Officer down!" she screamed. "I need help."

Jake put his hands on either side of her head and tapped her cheek. "Wake up, Abby," he commanded. "It's Jake. You're with me and you're safe." His tone softened. "It's just a dream, sweetheart. A bad dream." He repeated his words over and over until finally the rocking stopped.

But Abby's breathing was labored. To Jake it

sounded as if she was gasping for breath. Finally, a tiny voice said, "Jake?"

He squeezed her hands. "I'm right here, Abby. Right here."

Only then did her eyes open. Bigger and darker than he'd ever seen them. He continued to stroke her hands and murmur reassurances while he watched her gaze around the room until a frown line creased her forehead.

"Okay. I'll bite," she said. "What happened? And," she added with a raised eyebrow, "how'd you get in?"

"Let's call it a bad dream," he replied calmly. He retained her hands in his and unobtrusively measured her pulse rate. Almost normal. "What do you remember?" he prodded.

He watched her expressive face reflect her thoughts and knew the exact moment she figured out the puzzle. Her eyes widened, her complexion paled. Then she pushed herself into a sitting position and propped the pillows behind her. She took a deep breath and looked him square in the face.

"A bad dream?" she asked. "Or did I have another flashback, this time while I slept."

"What do you remember?" he asked again.

She frowned before she replied. "This is weird. I can't remember the scenes, but I remember the feelings all too well. Fright. Helplessness. Guilt." She wrapped her arms around herself. "The same emotions I had when I discovered Tom Conroy's body.'' Now she buried her head in her hands. ''Those feelings just won't go away.''

Jake pulled her into his arms, and she cuddled against his chest as though she'd done it a thousand times before. He kissed the top of her head, her cheek, her neck.

''Flashbacks are so awful,'' she began, speaking directly into his chest. ''It's like being there again, reliving everything. Every step I took, everything I saw and every emotion I felt. The horror and the feelings just won't stop.''

''It's been only a little over a month, Abby,'' he said gently. ''As usual, you're being too hard on yourself.''

She sighed, and finally leaned away, looking up at him as she answered. ''Maybe. But I need to put this behind me and move on, just like you said the other day. I've got to get back to normal soon.''

''I don't think recovery from psychological trauma has a set schedule. But you're the expert here. You tell me.''

''Gee whiz,'' she grumbled. ''You sound just like Martin.''

Jake breathed a sigh of relief. She sounded more like herself. His counseling skills were rusty, but at least he hadn't done any harm. ''You want to call him?''

''Who? Martin?''

He nodded.

"No." She shook her head. "Absolutely not."

"Why not?" asked Jake, surprised at her response. He thought Martin Bernstein was one of the good guys. "Dr. Bernstein will be able to help you a hell of a lot better than I can."

The smile she gave him was so sweet and loving, he knew he'd remember it forever. "You're doing a great job with me," she whispered. "And besides, if I confess to Martin that I've had two episodes in the short time I've been here, he'll probably tell me to come home."

CHAPTER ELEVEN

HOME? No-o! Jake's arms tightened automatically around Abby, who once again rested across his chest. Her sweet warmth permeated his body. "You don't really want to go back to California, do you?" He closed his eyes and held his breath while waiting for her answer.

"What do you think?" she mumbled into his pecs.

Her husky voice held a wealth of promise and his eyes snapped open...just in time to see a yawn overtake her. He stroked her hair and fought his quick arousal. It seemed a sleepy, tousled Abby appealed to him as much as a beautiful, alert Abby. Exasperated, he exhaled hard. He should be shot for his thoughts—making love to a woman who'd just woken up from a nightmare.

"You've had a rough time, sweetheart," he said. "Why don't I go home and let you sleep. In fact, sleep as late as you want and I'll get the kids off tomorrow."

He'd barely finished speaking when he felt her hands tighten on his waist. "Don't go."

He heard the fear in her voice. "No problem," he replied, leaning back against the pillows again, keeping Abby next to him. He smiled as he felt her body relax, felt the regularity of her breathing. A minute later, he saw her eyelids close as she fell asleep again.

A chuckle tickled his throat. He'd pictured Abby with him in bed dozens of times in the last few days. But not quite this way. He looked at her again, realizing she trusted him. Why else would she have asked him to stay? Why else would she have allowed herself to fall asleep in his arms?

He kissed her temple and pulled the bedspread higher to cover them both. One by one, his muscles relaxed as he continued to hold her. A sweet armful. He kissed her again. Oh, he could get used to this. Get used to Abby. He stared at her and his heart ricocheted. This woman was special in every wonderful way, but she'd been through so much. Could he ever hope to fill her heart and steer her mind to thoughts of a happy future? A future with him? His breath whooshed out of his lungs at the idea. A future with Abby felt right. Together they'd be able to handle everything—Stacey, families, careers, flashbacks.

But first, he'd have to get her to change her thinking. There was no way she was returning to Cali-

fornia in two months. Not if he could help it. His
grin turned into a laugh, a laugh at himself. Here he
was, making plans while Abby slept, totally unaware. Um…maybe not *totally* unaware, he admitted, looking at the woman who'd invited him to stay
the night.

His strategy would start with a great dinner at the
Whistling Swan on Friday night. And on Saturday
night, they'd share popcorn at the movies. And on
Sunday, well, he'd figure something out by then. He
was going to take her out, get her away from the
house and have fun. Alone. With him.

ON FRIDAY AFTERNOON Stacey leaned out of the
school bus and pointed at the blue car on the orchard
road. "Look, Cindy," she said to the girl next to
her, "Abby's waiting for us today."

"Who's Abby?" Cindy looked puzzled. "Is she
your mom? If I called my mom Nancy she'd *kill*
me."

Stacey giggled. Cindy was sort of an actress like
Aunt Maureen. And usually she was funny. Very
funny. That's why Stacey liked her so much.
"Abby's not my mom. She takes care of us and
she's really nice. You'll like her."

The bus stopped. Stacey stood up and turned
around. "Jon. Mac. Let's go." She rolled her eyes
at Cindy as the boys clambered past them. "Don't

mind the twins. Daddy says their noise lets us know where they are, so they can't get into real trouble."

This time Cindy giggled. "You're so lucky, Stacey. I wish I had some sisters or brothers." She sighed deeply. "You know what they say about being an only child, don't you?"

"Nope."

"Only...is...lonely." Cindy's voice quivered. She bent her head, her chin touching her chest.

Stacey studied her friend, for once unable to tell if she was kidding or not. She wanted Cindy to have a good time today! Not be sad.

Suddenly, however, her friend stood up straight and grinned. "But I've got every Barbie ever made. Daddy says he's glad that at least he doesn't have to share the bathroom with them!"

Stacey looked at Cindy's sparkling eyes and started to laugh. Then Cindy started to laugh. The longer Stacey looked at Cindy, the harder she laughed. Her sides began to hurt. Cindy kept on laughing, too. Stacey couldn't even walk to the car.

"Like a gaggle of giggling geese." Abby stood next to them, hands on her hips, a big grin on her face. "A very small gaggle of cute geese."

"Hi, Abby," Stacey finally said. "This is my friend, Cindy."

"Hi, Cindy. Welcome to Stacey's home. Now, what's so funny with you two?"

"Nothing!" said Stacey.

"Nothing!" said Cindy, but she burst out laughing again.

"Ahh," said Abby. "I think you're off to a great afternoon."

And she did have a great day with Cindy, thought Stacey three hours later, except when her friend asked about Claire. But she wasn't mad at Cindy or anything. Every kid is supposed to have a mom. So Cindy was only curious.

"Stace?" said Cindy as she'd stroked the new kittens in the barn.

"Yeah?"

"Abby's nice."

"I know. I like her."

"Does your dad like her?"

"Sure he does."

Cindy sighed one of her actress sighs. "But does he *like* her? You know what I mean."

Stacey had thought of the day her dad watched Abby and her do their aerobics. She nodded. "I once saw him look at her, and look at her, and look at her. He didn't even turn to look at me. And her skin started getting pink."

"Ahh! She blushed."

Stacey nodded. "Yeah, she did."

"So maybe she likes him too," said Cindy. "Maybe—"

"I don't think so," said Stacey quickly. "He

didn't say anything to me and my dad wouldn't keep that kind of secret.''

Cindy had just looked at her and then talked about how lucky Stacey was to live on the orchard with all the animals and trees and room to run around in.

She had agreed but she knew Cindy wouldn't want to trade places. Cindy had a mom.

ABBY HUMMED while she organized dinner for the family that evening. Stacey's happiness sent a warm glow through Abby, and she switched from humming to quiet singing.

For a woman who'd had a broken night's sleep, her energy seemed limitless today. Must be due to the second half of the night...the deep dreamless hours when Jake had been with her. Jake. She'd thought about him all day, and had walked around with a silly grin on her face.

She walked into the living room, and waved the children into the kitchen. ''I'll bring you a tray in here,'' she told Susan.

''Thanks, but I think I'll treat myself to a meal with the family.'' Susan swung her legs over the side of the couch. ''It's Friday night and I've been good all week.''

''Would Robert agree?'' asked Abby as she went to help the other woman stand up.

''Oh, my husband would *breathe* for me if I let him,'' laughed Susan, affection lacing her voice.

"These Templeton men," she continued as she stared hard at Abby, "are really special. Very devoted."

Abby paused.

"I'm a lucky woman," continued Susan, waddling slowly toward the kitchen.

Abby followed, glad her companion didn't seem to expect her to reply. Susan's comment, however, remained with her.

And then she spotted Jake, in profile, washing his hands at the sink and all thought fled as she stood quietly, absorbing his presence. Not only the picture he made in his short-sleeve jersey and snug jeans, but also the energy he exuded. The man was so alive!

He turned around and his face lit up when he saw her, as though she were the only woman in the world. She lost her breath.

"Don't even nibble," he warned her with a voice as sexy as sin in the city.

"What?" she whispered, confused.

He glanced at the pan of lasagna she had put on the table along with some fragrant garlic bread. "Save your appetite for later."

"How come Abby can't eat?" asked Stacey, sliding into her chair. "We've got plenty of food, and she'll be hungry all night."

"Great question," boomed Robert, walking into the kitchen and into the conversation. "We don't starve people we like." He winked at Abby and kissed his wife.

"The thing about this family," replied Jake, catching Abby's eye, "is that everybody has to know everything!" He walked across the room and stood beside her. "I'm not starving her. I'm taking her to dinner later in town...where there's peace and quiet."

Two seconds of silence greeted his statement. Then Jon spoke. "We could be quiet, Uncle Jake, if we had lots of candy to eat."

"Yeah, maybe chocolate bars and...Gummi Bears! I love Gummi Bears the best." Mac's big blue eyes widened even more.

"So, Daddy," said the third child, a thoughtful expression on her face, "are you and Abby going on a date?"

Stacey's question brought Abby's reverie to a screeching halt. How could she have forgotten Stacey? The sensitive girl would have feelings about this.

"Actually, Stacey," she began. "We're—"

"Abby and I are going out for a nice quiet grown-up dinner," said Jake, smiling at his daughter. "We won't be home for a while."

Abby held her breath as Stacey listened to her dad, then watched as the girl studied Jake.

"But Abby's *my* friend," said Stacey, the corners of her lips quivering.

"Of course she is," replied Jake, taking a seat next to his daughter. "That won't change, I promise you."

"You promise?" Stacey looked at Jake. "The cross-your-heart-and-hope-to-die kind of promise?"

"Absolutely."

Stacey turned to Abby. "Are you going to promise, too?"

Abby crossed her heart.

"Okay," Stacey said. "Then I guess it's all right. But Daddy—" she narrowed her eyes and frowned as she examined Jake from head to toe "—you can't go like that. You're so grungy, Abby won't want to be seen with you!"

From fear to enthusiasm in mere seconds, Stacey's reactions rode on the surface for all to see. Susan and Robert didn't try to hide their grins. Elinor also smiled. The twins were quiet as they looked at the adults. Abby watched them absorb the vibrations in the room and wondered what would come out of their mouths.

"Hey, Stacey," said Jon, bouncing on his chair, "if your dad and Abby go on lots of dates, maybe Abby can be your new mother."

"Yeah," added Mac. "Then you'll have two. One here and one in heaven. Good idea. Ask Uncle Jake if he'll let her be your mom."

Abby's breath caught; she felt heat rise to her face even as a corner of her heart ripped. Robert, also, looked distressed. But Stacey seemed merely thoughtful as she turned to her cousins.

"That's really a dumb idea," she finally said. "It can't happen because Daddy and Abby would have to fall in love. And I don't think they can because Daddy loves Mommy." She paused for a moment, a crease lining her young forehead. "Right, Daddy?"

And Abby needed to escape. She spun toward Jake. "I'll let you handle the questions." She waved to everyone as she left the room. Then she stuck her head back in. "One more thing. Pile the dishes in the sink. Jake will handle them, too."

JAKE WATCHED Abby's hurried retreat, frustrated that he couldn't be in two places at once, but very aware that his conversation with Stacey now could affect the future of all three of them. He smiled at his daughter, sat on the chair next to her and pulled her into his lap.

"Come here, Pumpkin, and let's talk."

"Okay. Sometimes I get tired of thinking so much by myself."

Her words squeezed his heart, and when she leaned back against him so trustingly, tears stung his eyes. He kissed her quickly on the forehead before he began speaking.

"Your mommy was a very special lady, Stace, and we'll always love her," he said slowly. "She's part of you and she's part of me, and she always will be. Understand?''

Stacey nodded.

"We'll never forget her, Stacey. Never." Jake had to clear his throat to continue. "Look across at your cousins. How many boys do you see?"

"Two."

"Right. There are two of them. Do you think Uncle Robert and Aunt Sue love only Mac? Or love only Jon?"

Stacey stared at the boys without blinking. Jake looked down at her face, could almost feel her thought waves vibrating as she made connections. He pressed on.

"And when the new baby comes, won't they love her as well?"

She nodded.

"The secret is that love grows, Pumpkin. Our hearts pump as much love as we need to give, so we never run out of it. And that's why I would be able to love Abby and still love Mommy. And it's okay." He kissed her again and whispered, "Do you understand what I'm saying?"

She nodded, then turned her face into his chest. "But, what if...you love Abby and Abby doesn't love me?"

Jake smiled at the impossibility. "I don't think you need to worry about that."

"Yes I do. You don't understand...." Her hand instinctively covered her stomach.

"What's wrong, Pumpkin? What are you thinking?" He hadn't seen that gesture in a while and had hoped it was a thing of the past.

Stacey shook her head. "I can't tell," she whispered. "But maybe Abby won't love me. Maybe she *shouldn't* love me."

"My darling daughter," Jake whispered, "you deserve the love of the entire world, no matter what you think. Don't you know how easy it is to love you?" He wrapped her in his arms.

Stacey lingered a moment, then squirmed from his lap and faced him, running a critical eye up and down. "If you're really going on a date with Abby, then you'd better dress up and look nice." She ran her palm over his cheek. "And take a shave, and, and...bring her flowers." Her eyes shone at the thought. "Yes, ladies like flowers."

He glanced at his mother and Susan.

"Oh, ladies like flowers," echoed Elinor, beaming at her granddaughter.

Susan laughed, then added, "You did well, Jakey. You sure do know how to handle hearts! Now just cut a few mums from outside and you'll make two ladies happy."

ABBY WELCOMED the cool air on her face as soon as she escaped the kitchen. The fall evenings were wonderful, she thought as she walked back to her cottage. The weather. Great. So now she was focusing on the weather, always a safe diversion from the real questions in life.

They'd cancel their dinner plans. She'd tell Jake she'd changed her mind when he came to get her. *If* he came to get her. In the meantime, she needed a shower. A long, cool shower.

Maybe she should have stayed to talk with Stacey. Without meaning to, Jake often said the wrong thing to the girl, like threatening to call her school or suggesting dancing classes. She reached the small house and let herself inside, her mind still whirling.

What had she been thinking? How could she possibly go on a date with Jake or contemplate any meaningful involvement with him when his daughter was so vulnerable? She couldn't.

Well, she'd tell Jake when she saw him again. In the meantime, she needed that shower desperately. She grabbed clean undies and her long chenille robe and headed for the bathroom.

The knock came when she was toweling dry. She jammed her arms into the sleeves of her robe, tightened the belt and strode to the door. She opened it. And there was Jake.

"Everything's cool," he began without waiting for her to ask. "I talked to Stacey and she talked to me—up to a point. But in the end, this was her idea." Jake handed her a bouquet of flowers.

She heard the words without comprehending them, but managed to reach for the flowers. Roses, chrysanthemums, sunflowers, familiar varieties that beautified the grounds around the house. "From Stacey and her dad," Jake reiterated. "Look up at me, Abby."

Easy enough. She couldn't have turned away if she'd wanted to. With his observant eyes matching his open-collared blue dress shirt, sleeves casually rolled up to below the elbow, he made her mouth water. Until she remembered the resolution she'd made less than an hour ago.

"What were you saying about Stacey?" she asked.

He smiled. "She's great. Almost. I'll give you the details later."

She was about to reply, when she saw an awareness in his expression as he studied her, as though he'd just realized she wore nothing beneath the robe. She saw heat fill his eyes. She felt heat scorch her face. For an instant, she wanted to run. Instead, she planted her feet and met his gaze. "Tell me what happened after I left. If my going out with you is going to cause Stacey more stress, then I can't—"

His demeanor changed. A smile played at the corner of his mouth. His eyes began to twinkle and the sexual passion transformed itself into a deep warmth, a warmth infused with…happiness…and…more…

Love. She saw it. He didn't try to hide it. All breath escaped her lungs, and she couldn't move.

Jake had no problem moving. He walked into the cottage and gathered her into his arms, held her snugly, then covered her mouth with his own.

Her mind flooded with impressions of Jake. The sight, the smell, the taste of him. But most of all the touch. She came to life when he kissed her. She loved the feel of his lips on hers, of his hands stroking the hollow of her back, and then, when he lifted his head to look at her, his large palm caressing her face as though it were the most delicate crystal ever created. His intense expression told its own story. To her dismay, she felt tears fill the corners of her eyes.

"Oh, God, Abby. Don't cry." The horror in Jake's voice was the best prescription for stopping the overflow.

"Okay," she agreed in a small voice. "Jake," she whispered, meeting his gaze. "Jake—"

"Shh…" he said quietly, putting a gentle finger over her mouth. "You don't have to say a word. I didn't mean to cause you distress. I just wanted you to know—"

"I do know," she replied with a wobbly smile. She reached for his hands and squeezed them. "I was on track for a simple relationship, but now my head's spinning. Nothing is ever simple, is it?"

He shook his head. "And nothing worthwhile is ever easy."

He had that right.

SURPRISINGLY, SHE ENJOYED her dinner. The Whistling Swan offered fine dining downstairs with casual fare served in the Ugly Duckling Loft.

"I had a long, leisurely meal in mind," Jake had said when they entered the restaurant, his fingers intertwined with hers. "A table for two. You and I. Alone." He'd turned to her. "I thought we'd stay down here."

"Fine. Just fine." In fact, she'd thought it more than fine. Was this their first time together without the cast of thousands in the background? Sure, they'd taken nightly walks at the orchard, but this evening was different. No children, no family, no business interruptions. Just themselves.

They followed the waiter to a quiet table and ordered two glasses of red wine. Abby sat back and looked across at Jake. "This restaurant is lovely," she said, "but getting away for one evening is even better."

"Then let's make a pact not to discuss the orchard, the family or anything connected to them," said Jake. "Let's make this a real get-away-from-it-all event."

Abby laughed. "We may run out of things to talk about," she teased.

"I doubt that," Jake replied, as he reached to cover Abby's hand with his.

Two hours later, Abby glanced at her watch and was stunned to see how much time had passed. Jake had been right. Conversation between them had flowed easily. Even now, Jake was in the middle of telling her about his job.

"I'm due at the hospital on Tuesday just for the day," he said as his fingers caressed hers across the tabletop. "Connie, my secretary, called me today. Big powwow about the new lab." Excitement made his eyes glow. "This research is going to make a real difference," he said. "We are going to affect— in a big way—the treatment of cardiovascular disease and advanced coronary disease."

His work meant so much to him, just as mine used to mean the world to me. Suddenly unsettled, Abby banished the last part of the thought as quickly as it came, and squeezed Jake's hand. "I'm glad for you. The recognition is nice, but the work itself means everything."

He sat straighter. "It means a hell of a lot, but not quite everything, sweetheart. Especially now." His loving smile was dangerous to her peace of mind. Dangerous to her heart. She was becoming addicted to those smiles.

To release the sudden tension, she patted her stomach. "Great dessert," she said with a grin as she lifted her coffee cup.

"Hmm…" He nodded.

It wasn't hard figuring out what Jake wanted for dessert. She looked into his face and knew that she wanted him as much as he wanted her. She put her cup down before the coffee could spill.

So what did it mean, this feeling of breathlessness, her damp hands, and the silly grin always trying to emerge whenever she thought about him? The "L" word came to mind, but did she really want to admit it? No. She didn't. Just as she avoided thinking about her job, she didn't want to think about her feelings toward Jake either. Too confusing. What a coward she was! Her expertise at hiding from herself was growing.

"Ready?" Jake inquired. "Or is there one more chocolate morsel to be eaten?" He shook his head in mock reproach. "Your secret's out, Abby. I know why you exercise so much. You'll do anything for chocolate." He rose from his seat and walked behind her chair.

Tilting her head, she returned his smile as she stood up. "Aerobic activity does keep the weight down, but mainly I feel like a million bucks after a workout. Of course," she added, "I may look like a dishrag, but it's worth it."

He signed for the check, took her arm and guided her from the room. "Trust me," he said. "I've seen you after a workout and dishrag is the last thing I'd call you."

"Well, Stacey calls us 'sweathogs.'"

His laughter sounded like the music of Niagara Falls—powerful and exciting. "She's happy with you, is all," he finally replied.

"I hope so," said Abby.

"I know so," Jake replied as they reached his Subaru. He opened the passenger door while she slid into the seat and buckled her belt. When she looked up at him, he leaned in and kissed her before closing the door and walking to his side of the vehicle.

A quick kiss. That's all it took for her heart to beat double time and her thoughts to race ahead.

THE EVENING wasn't over, and he didn't want to talk about Stacey right then. He didn't want to think about her. Tonight he wasn't a father. He was a man. A man who loved the woman sitting next to him. A man who wanted to make love to her until they both lost their minds.

He glanced to the side, wishing the bucket seats would disappear so she could sit closer. With his eyes on the darkened road, he reached for her hand, enjoying the contact, the feel of her smooth skin on his own.

"Ah, Jake," sighed Abby, inching a trifle closer within the confines of her seat.

"Ah, Abby," he mimicked, lifting her hand to kiss her fingers. "What are you thinking about, sweetheart?"

"Oh, just life."

"Small topic," he joked. "Sounds provocative."

"Not quite," she replied. "It's just...I am such an idiot!"

"Hey," he replied, trying not to laugh. "Don't talk about my special date that way!"

"Ja—cob." Her voice softened, turned sultry as she melted his name into soft, sweet caramel.

His antennae rose. "What, darling?"

"Why don't you use that accelerator and get us home?"

The car shot forward.

CHAPTER TWELVE

SHE FELT comfortable with his arm around her as they walked to the cottage, as they climbed the two steps until they reached the door. He turned toward her then, searching her face, looking hard…and at last he leaned forward, his hands light on her shoulders.

She wanted his kiss. But she wanted more. She studied him too, his smoldering blue eyes, his intensity as he feasted his gaze on her. His light touch sent her heart shooting the rapids, and then she knew the truth. Her heart was his.

She loved him.

She loved him even though she wasn't ready. Even though she hadn't been looking for love. Even though this certainly wasn't the best time in her life to discover love. *But maybe there never was a best time.* Maybe the secret was to recognize love whenever it appeared and embrace it.

The soft touch of his lips ignited a flame inside her. She raised to her toes, arms locking around his neck, her mouth answering his call. "Let's go inside," she gasped when she could breathe again.

"Thought you'd never ask," Jake whispered against her hair as he took the key from her trembling fingers.

He locked the door behind him and held out his hand. "Look at this," he said quietly. "My hand's not a hundred percent steady either."

She was touched by Jake's sensitivity. "It's been a long time," Abby whispered, her eyes avoiding his. "A very long time."

"That's nothing to be embarrassed about."

Maybe not, Abby acknowledged silently, but she'd probably make an idiot of herself, awkward and unsure at the very least.

"Lift those pansy eyes my way, sweetheart," said Jake, taking her in his arms. "You're a beautiful woman, with a beautiful heart. There's nothing you can do that could change the way I feel." His lips touched hers like a whisper and she kissed him with a hunger that shocked her down to her toes. She couldn't stop. Her mind whirled. And when he crushed her to him, there was nowhere else on earth she wanted to be.

Except in his bed. Making love all night.

JAKE SCOOPED ABBY into his arms and walked toward the bedroom. What he'd done to deserve her, he didn't know. All he knew was when he looked into her eyes, he saw the love she had for him. When he kissed her, when he held her, she turned to flame. He nuzzled her neck and inhaled her special scent. Some men never found love even once, and he'd been blessed twice. Twice in a lifetime.

He eased her onto the queen-size bed, his heart full when she opened her arms to him. Her eyes were darker than night, her lips swollen from kissing him. She might have been the epitome of every man's dream—sensuous, sultry and seductive—but she was very real to him. Trusting, caring and challenging. As real and solid as his own heartbeat. And he cherished every aspect of her.

"We can take it as slowly as you like," he whispered as he rained kisses on the corners of her mouth, her neck, and then back to her tempting lips.

"I don't think so," Abby gasped, grabbing the front of his shirt and quickly releasing the buttons.

Her eagerness affected him instantly, and he was ready to love her too soon. Much too soon. "Easy, baby, easy," he crooned more for his own sake than for hers. He leaned over her, one hand playing with the bottom of her silk ribbed sweater. He inched it higher and to his delight, Abby helped him scoop it up over her head.

The delicate lace of her bra blended with her creamy skin so that her full breasts tantalized him behind their sheer screen. He traced the edge of the lace with his tongue, over the swell of her breast, into the crevice and again higher, tasting silky skin. His tongue continued traveling, now on top of the lace, and paused at the peak, gently teasing the nipple.

"Oh, Jake..." Wonder in her voice, heat in her eyes.

And they'd barely started.

"Jake?"

"Right here, darling."

"Take the damn thing off!"

"My pleasure," he chuckled as he finally unhooked the bra's front clasp and viewed the gift he'd unwrapped. The gift she'd offered him.

He reached for her hand. "You're so beautiful, Abby," he said in a voice hoarse with emotion. He touched his lips to her dusky pink nipples.

Abby writhed instantly, had to grip the bedspread to keep herself anchored to earth. She wasn't beautiful, but she felt that way every time Jake touched her, every time he kissed her and drove her mindless.

"Take off your shirt," she panted, reaching to help him. "I want to touch...you." She stroked his chest, enjoying the rough sensation of his hair against her palms. Her fingers grazed his nipples, and she heard his quick intake of breath.

"You're right," Jake murmured. "This isn't a slow boat to China."

In a flash, her pants hit the floor, his slacks on top

of them a moment later. She reached for him, wanting his chest on hers, his mouth on hers, and she didn't want to wait. She didn't have to.

When he kissed her this time, she pressed her open lips to his and welcomed him inside, never wanting the kiss to end. But then his hand began strumming her body, composing melodies she'd never heard before, creating a rhythm just for two. Sensations swarmed her. She couldn't think! Her breath turned to gasps, and she trembled on the verge of meltdown. His hand paused on her hip, on the elastic of her undies.

"You don't need these anymore," he whispered. "May I?"

Speechless, she nodded and then returned the favor.

"Hold me, Jake. Hurry!"

"Glad to oblige, but there's no hurry, is there?" His breathless voice betrayed his teasing words.

He entered her. And there were no more words.

WOULD SHE ever breathe normally again? Abby lay with her head on Jake's shoulder, peeping at him from beneath her lashes, pleased to note he hadn't caught his breath yet either. She closed her eyes, savoring the wonder of her discovery. Treasuring it.

She bit her lip. How would she turn her back on this in November? She'd think about it later.

"Um," Abby murmured as she snuggled closer,

listening to Jake's heart beating strongly beneath her ear. "Are you back on earth yet?"

Jake chuckled and stroked her arm. "Good question. After that experience, I'm anyplace you are, sweetheart."

His confession touched her heart and her eyes felt moist. "I'll admit," she said, "that making love with you was unique for me. And I'll also admit," she added with a laugh, "that I'm glad there's a queen-size bed in here. For a lean sort of guy, you take up a lot of room."

"Sweetie, an army cot wouldn't have stopped me. I've been wanting to make love to you from the beginning."

"Liar! You wanted me evicted when we met."

"Maybe. But that was before I got to know you," Jake replied.

"And I wanted to leave."

"But not anymore." His voice held a faint question.

Abby paused before answering, aware that "thinking about it later" had become sooner. "Want to leave? No. But I've got some things to work out, Jake. It's more than just coping with flashbacks… it's figuring out how to go on helping people when I can't seem to help myself. I've wanted to be a psychologist my entire life, but if I can't be effective…then what's the point? This is important to me.

I can't run away from it. So before I can go on with
my life, I have to come to terms…face the fear…''

"In California?''

"Yes, I think so,'' came her careful reply. She
caressed his face, the strong jaw, the high cheekbones. "So, to use a cliché, I suggest we just 'seize
the day' one at a time.''

Jake didn't respond right away.

"So what do you think about my idea?'' Abby
asked, her fingers roaming the expanse of his chest.

He loved her touch on his skin, but if she kept it
up he wouldn't be able to think at all.

"If we seize the day,'' he replied, "we should
seize the night as well.'' He touched his lips to hers,
traced them with his tongue, and her response was
everything he could have hoped for.

And then he couldn't reason at all. Not when
Abby squirmed beneath him, not when her arms
tightened around him, not when her every reaction
to his touch sent him spinning.

"I love you, Abigail,'' he whispered.

She moaned this time and pulled him closer once
again. And he made love to her once more.

"THAT WAS EVEN MORE…special than the first
time.''

Abby's contentment, coupled with a sense of
wonder, lingered in her voice, and Jake tucked his
arm around her, enjoying her presence in every way.

She was a perfect match for him. She'd followed his lead...when he wasn't following hers. A perfect partnership.

"Making love gets better all the time," he replied to Abby's remark, his hands playing with her wavy hair. "It's as natural as breathing and a hell of a lot more fun."

She chuckled and Jake joined in, once again convinced that Abby was made for him. Then she reached for his hand and squeezed it gently.

"So are you going to tell me how you handled the kids after I escaped the kitchen this evening? Between the twins' ideas of how to acquire a mom and Stacey needing to figure out how love works, I bet you had your hands full."

He bestowed a quick kiss on her smiling mouth before he answered. He loved seeing her relaxed and laughing.

"I may have carried the ball, but I wasn't exactly alone," Jake explained. "The entire clan was there, hanging on to every word."

"Poor Jake! No privacy."

He snorted. "Privacy? My family doesn't know what the word means." His fingertips stroked her arm, traveled to her hand and clasped it. "But in this case, privacy didn't matter because where Stacey is concerned, they all have to know what's going on. When I'm in Boston, they're in charge."

"That makes sense," agreed Abby.

"Tonight was the first time Stacey's seen me go out with a woman other than her mom," he began, "and she was confused."

Abby stayed silent.

"So I unconfused her."

"I'm all ears."

In ten minutes, Jake gave Abby a succinct playback of his dialogue with Stacey. "Everything went well until the end when she said that maybe you wouldn't or couldn't love her. What really got me was when she starting rubbing her stomach again." He sighed deeply. "So there's still something eating away at her."

"Yes," agreed Abby. "But the desire to be happy is also driving her now. There are cracks in her defenses. She laughs. She's made a friend. She brought the friend home and they had a great time. She talked about Claire." Abby twisted around in his arms until she faced him. She put her hands on either side of his face, capturing his attention. "Jake, she wants to move forward. She does."

"And all because of you," he said. "And I thank you from the bottom of my heart."

"Don't," said Abby, putting a finger over his mouth. "I've only played a small part. You've played a much bigger one. You're her dad. You've been home full-time this week. Don't you think she's reacting to that? Don't you think she's happier when you're around?"

Pain almost prevented him from answering. His lips pressed together, his eyes closed for a moment. "I don't really know," he whispered.

"Jake!" Abby protested. "She loves you."

"Yeah." He nodded. "She does. But...there's something else." He'd never articulated his fear before and could barely say the words aloud even now. But he trusted Abby. He took a steadying breath. "I think for some reason she's also afraid of me...afraid of me!...her own dad...or afraid of something that has to do with me. I've tried everything I can to reassure her, but obviously I'm missing something. So when you ask me if she's happier when I'm around, the truthful answer is, I don't know."

ABBY SHOULD HAVE SLEPT like the proverbial log after Jake left in the wee hours of the morning. Making love with him had turned her limbs to rubber bands. Instead, however, she tossed on the bed, constantly shifting positions, her mind jumping to Stacey, to Jake, to the Templeton family and the myriad relationships that bound them. In a way, Stacey had too many bosses, when all she yearned for was one. Her dad. Why was she afraid?

Abby's thoughts wandered to her family in California, to Martin Bernstein, to her job, until finally, she felt herself drift off, falling, falling, almost falling asleep but not quite. Then suddenly big Tom

Conroy loomed in front of her, his mouth working, his face a picture of agony with tears running down his cheeks.

"It's all my fault, Doc. I killed that kid. I didn't mean to but I did. It's my fault. Can you help me?"

His voice seemed distorted. It seemed to echo from a distance, yet they were facing each other in her office. "Sit down, Tom," she said, indicating the visitor's chair, "and we'll work it out together."

He remained standing, however, just staring at her with pain-filled eyes. "You're a nice lady, Dr. MacKenzie," he said, drawing out the words, "but we both know you can't help. Nobody can help me. We can't undo it. And it's all my fault."

"You were in a terrible situation," she began, "people everywhere, a mad gunman in a crowd..."

"I killed a little boy. That's all I know." The tears had stopped, his face showed nothing. Even worse, his voice had emptied of all emotion. But his right hand tapped his holster, then clasped his gun.

Her heart raced. Her armpits felt wet. She knew what would happen next. She jumped from her chair. "No, Tom. No. Your family needs you. People love you. It wasn't your fault..."

He drew his gun and jerked his head to the side, "I left a note there...."

Horrified, she watched him raise the weapon and put the nozzle into his mouth. "No, Tom!" she screamed. "No-o-o-o...."

"No, no, no," she cried, sitting up in bed. She was shaking, sweating. She looked around her, her trembling hand on her chest feeling her heart beat out of control. She took a deep breath, then another. Tears dripped onto her nightgown. She raised her knees and wrapped her arms around them.

Only one person could be blamed for Tom's death. And that was Abby. If she thought she could escape the blame by taking a trip cross-country, she'd deluded herself. She'd never escape the nightmare, so she'd have to live with it.

THE NIGHTMARE HAD SHAKEN HER, but she took a shower and pasted a smile on her face before walking to the big house an hour later to prepare breakfast. Fortunately, Saturday was a busy day at the orchard and everyone would be occupied. She entered the kitchen, and immediately three pairs of bright blue eyes looked up at her.

"How was the date, Abby?" asked Stacey.

"Did ya' like the flowers? We helped Uncle Jake pick 'em."

She should have expected an interrogation from the kids. What had happened to her great idea of a relaxing change of pace, where she could hide away in an apple orchard and just pick the darn apples? She sighed, knowing very well that she couldn't hide from her problems in an orchard or anywhere else.

"The date was fine, and I liked the flowers," said

Abby, swooping down to give each child a kiss on the cheek.

"Yuck," said Mac.

"What'd you do that for, Abby?" asked Jon, rubbing the kiss away.

"Because she likes us," said Stacey. "Don't you, Abby?"

"Of course I do. Who wouldn't like a group of such helpful children who know how to run an orchard and pick flowers for their uncle?"

The boys started to preen, and Abby winked at Stacey, before the girl could put her cousins down. Stacey smiled and nodded, her cheeks turning a faint pink.

"You look happy today, Stace," said Abby. "And so pretty."

"Thank you," she said, blushing harder. "I *am* happy today, Abby. Everything is good."

"Like what?" Abby probed.

"Like, you and Daddy had a date, and Daddy's home for another week, and Cynthia's coming over today, but she wants me to call her Cindy, and we'll have so many customers today and, I don't know…just everything is good today." She looked at Abby square in the eye. "I just wish it could be like this every day."

Abby squeezed her hand and gave her another kiss. "Maybe it can, darling. Maybe soon you'll feel good every day." And maybe Jake had been wrong about his daughter. Stacey certainly seemed happier when he was around.

"Can we have pancakes, Abby? I don't want bagels anymore."

"Sure, Jon. I'll make a big batch for the whole family."

"See," said Stacey. "It's a really good day."

Just then Susan and Robert walked into the kitchen. Susan seemed more uncomfortable than ever, her legs swollen, her movements slow. Abby determined to keep a closer eye on the woman whom she'd come to like so much.

"I just don't understand it," said Susan. "I don't remember being this uncomfortable with the twins, and I was bigger than I am now."

"I hate to break this to you, my darling," replied Robert, "but you're a few years older now—still gorgeous—but older."

"Older? Moi? Well, maybe true," Susan admitted with a sly grin, "but no matter how old I get, my darling, I can't seem to catch up with you!"

Abby chuckled at their byplay, admiring the relationship they had.

"You'll pay later, sweets, you'll pay," growled Robert in a mock-threatening manner as he kissed his wife on the cheek. "In the meantime," he said, gently leading her to a chair, "you'll sit quietly and eat something."

"And on Monday," came Jake's voice from the threshold, "you'll visit your doctor."

Susan's eyes narrowed as she glared at the brothers. "You're both too bossy. And why, for heaven's sake, should I see my doctor on Monday when my appointment's in two weeks?" She aimed that question at Jake.

Jake sauntered to where the woman sat, and casually picked up her hand and studied his watch. "Your pulse is fast, Susie, your legs are twice their normal size, so you're going to the doctor in two days, not two weeks."

"Oh, dear," she replied with a quick change in attitude. "What are we afraid of, Jakey?"

"Nothing we can't handle. Could be a little toxemia building up, which means your blood pressure can rise. Happens sometimes with pregnant women. So, we'll just stay on top of it."

Abby watched as Susan cradled her stomach in the way pregnant women often did. Abby would do the same if anything threatened her baby. Instinctively, she glanced at Jake, and found his eyes on her. She felt heat rise to her cheeks and looked away before he could see the blush. How stupid of her to think about such things. Especially when she still carried around so much guilt that her dreams turned to nightmares. She shivered as she recalled her latest one, then walked to the counter, eager to prepare those pancakes.

"Morning, sweetheart."

Abby whirled to find Jake standing right behind her. "Good morning."

His eyes examined, his forehead wrinkled. "What's wrong?"

Did he have mental telepathy or was she so poor an actress? Abby smiled. "You startled me. That's all."

He shook his head. "I don't think so." He took her hand in his warm, steady one, and she felt calmer. Then he leaned in to whisper, "Having second thoughts the morning after?"

Second thoughts? Now her smile came easily. "Not one," she replied, reaching for a mixing bowl.

"Good. So what's wrong?" he repeated.

"Nothing that can't be fixed. It's just that I need to call Martin."

He clasped her shoulders, pulled her close and held her. "Another flashback? When?"

"A nightmare early this morning." She stepped out of his arms. "Hand me the pancake mix, the eggs and the milk while you're standing here. Good. Make yourself useful."

"I should have stayed the night," he said, passing her the items.

"It wouldn't have made a difference. You can't protect me from my dreams, or from myself," she replied. "I've got to take control of this."

Jake looked across the room at his daughter, then

looked at Abby. "Seems to me I'm not too good at protecting anybody from anything around here. I do much better work at the hospital. It's a lot easier over there."

"You're a gifted doctor, Jake. Your patients are lucky to have you."

"And yours couldn't ask for a more caring, talented person than you."

Abby concentrated on mixing the batter with a wooden spoon and ignored Jake's remark. He now saw her through rose-colored glasses. Everyone tended to see those they loved as better than they were. She paused as a grin spread across her face. If that's how love worked, was it really so bad?

"Hold that thought!" said Jake. "I don't know what's going on inside your head, but—" he gave her a quick kiss "—I love seeing that smile."

"Don't worry, Jake. I'll work it all out."

An hour later, the kitchen emptied, and silence settled over the room with such speed, Abby's ears echoed. "Wow!" she said to Susan when the two women were alone. "It's unnerving."

"Don't question it, just enjoy it. Peace and quiet don't often inhabit this house."

"But you love it," said Abby. "All of it."

Susan's face softened, her eyes looked dreamy. "Wouldn't trade a thing. Not even the noise." She studied Abby carefully. "I've known Jake a long time, Abby. I really do love him as a brother and

I'd like nothing better than to see him happy again. Are you the woman who's going to get him there?''

Abby recognized Susan's sincerity, despite her personal question. So Abby answered with total candor. ''I know what you want to hear, Susan, but my answer is, I don't know. I just don't know.''

''So does that mean you're going to wind up hurting him?''

''Do you think I want to?'' Abby snapped. ''But my answer to this question is the same as to your first—I just don't know.''

A heartbeat passed. ''Well, I know something,'' said Susan.

''What's that?''

''I'm going to have a baby,'' she replied. ''Right now.''

CHAPTER THIRTEEN

TWO HOURS LATER, the phone in the country store rang as Abby stood behind the cash register greeting customers and ringing up sales. Aunt Maureen, who'd hustled down when Abby called her, and the hired staff had managed to cover all aspects of the orchard's operations. Her old partner, Lucy, was driving the hay wagon instead of Jake. Stacey, Cynthia and the boys were at the petting zoo.

Abby held the phone to her ear, eager for news from the hospital front. "Hello."

"Hi, Abby. It's Jake. I'm at the hospital and everyone's okay now. We have a little girl."

His voice sounded hoarse but excited.

"Tell me about her," she invited, smiling at the customer in front of her. "Here's your change and thank you."

"I delivered her in the car."

"What did you say? In the car?" She almost dropped the phone.

"You heard me. This baby was in such a hurry, we couldn't get to the hospital. But Susan was terrific. Good thing she'd insisted on taking towels and blankets with us. Poor Rob was shaking so badly he couldn't keep the car on the road. So we parked and had a baby—a small baby—and then continued to the hospital, where mother and child are doing fine."

"How small?"

"Exactly four pounds," Jake replied. "Not too bad for an early bird. She's in an incubator, of course, with an IV for nourishment, but they'll try a bottle, too. Other than that, she's perfect. Heart is strong, lungs are working."

"Whew!" Abby released the breath she'd been holding. "That's wonderful news. So what happens now?"

"Rob needs to see the boys, and I need to see you. We're coming home."

Special words, Abby thought as she became aware of the next customer in line. "We just had a baby," she explained. "Elinor is a grandma again. Sorry for the delay." She packed the woman's purchases as quickly as she could before her thoughts drifted back to Jake.

He *needed* to see her.

The store had emptied out. Abby grabbed a piece of paper, glanced at her watch and put a sign on the door: Back at Noon. Then she went to find Elinor, Maureen and the children.

She spotted the two women hugging each other in the parking lot and joined them.

"So Susan's bed rest paid off," Maureen was saying. "Four pounds is giant-size in the neonatal unit."

"You're right. And we've been through this with the twins." Elinor's smile radiated warmth on everyone. "Come on. Let's go tell the children the news."

Abby fell into step next to Jake's mother just as Elinor turned to her friend. "This is turning out to be a terrific year, Maureen," she said. "Sending Abby to us was a stroke of genius. Jake is almost his old self again, Stacey is smiling, and we have a new baby."

"That may be true," said Abby with a grin, "but I didn't have anything to do with that last one!"

Elinor patted her on the arm. "That's okay, dear. The first two are more than enough."

Abby really had to set them straight. They were galloping into the sunset while she was just viewing the dawn. "Please don't get carried away, ladies. I'm only visiting. My home's in California. Remember?"

"Oh, fiddle-dee-dee," replied Elinor. "I've learned in life, dear, that 'Home is where the heart is.' It's an old cliché, but it's true. Didn't Maureen stay in Massachusetts because of Frank even though the rest of her family went West?"

"Tell you what," said Abby, wanting to end the conversation, "*if* I decide to do any relocating, you'll both be the first to know. How's that?"

Elinor turned to Maureen. "I think your niece just told us to mind our own business."

Maureen nodded. "She did it politely though, didn't she?"

"She's showing respect for the elderly."

Abby burst out laughing. "Elderly? Do you see any elderly folk around here? I sure don't. You can't be talking about yourselves. One of you runs a huge business. The other stars in full-length musicals. I can't keep up with you two."

"And so smart," added Maureen with a wink. "Knows just what to say to make us feel good."

"I give up," said Abby. "Let's go find the kids."

LAMBS, GOATS, RABBITS and ducklings were in outdoor pens in front of a small barn. Abby saw Jon and Mac chatting with visiting children and their parents. Cindy, Stacey's friend, had her arm around one of the lambs, but Stacey sat alone on a bale of hay, elbows on her knees, chin resting in her hands.

Abby quickened her step. Had Stacey and Cindy had a fight? Or was something else on Stacey's mind?

"Hi, everybody," said Abby.

Stacey's head snapped up, fear mixed with eagerness in her eyes.

"We have good news," Abby said quickly, relieved to see Stacey's fear dissipate a bit as the girl ran toward her.

"How's Aunt Sue?" Stacey's voice quavered as she spoke.

Abby pulled the girl into her arms, her heart squeezing at the child's anxiety. "She's fine, Stacey, just fine. Resting in the hospital."

Stacey leaned into Abby, but now looked toward Elinor. "Gram?"

"Abby's right, darling. Aunt Susan will be coming home in a few days."

Suddenly, Abby felt Stacey's full weight in her arms and she clasped the girl more firmly. "She's okay, sweetheart. Your aunt is one hundred percent fine. But you worried a whole lot, didn't you?"

Stacey nodded. "You never know sometimes, what's going to happen in an emergency," she whispered.

"That's true," Abby acknowledged. "But we always do the best we can, and this time, we were prepared."

"We were?"

"We sure were. Your grandma can tell you."

Elinor reached for Stacey's hands. "Your daddy, *the* Dr. Jacob Templeton, was with Aunt Sue and Uncle Rob and he delivered the baby in the car!"

Stacey's eyes shone. "Wow!"

"Come over here, boys, and let me tell you about

your new sister," continued Elinor, holding out her arms to the twins.

"A sister? We really got a girl baby?" asked Jon, running toward Elinor.

"Are you sure, Gram?" interrupted Mac. "'Cause we really need another brother for ball games."

Elinor beamed at them. "Boys, we have a little baby girl who's just beautiful."

"But you haven't seen her, Grandma," protested Jon. "Maybe she's ugly."

"Ugly?" asked Elinor in a voice laced with disbelief. "Not in this family! All my grandchildren are beautiful, even you, Jon!"

"Yuck! I'm not beautiful, Gram. I'm handsome!"

Abby shook her head, enjoying the discussion. She saw Elinor glance at Stacey and both roll their eyes in exactly the same way before producing identical grins.

"Listen carefully, children," continued Elinor. "You boys have a beautiful little sister, and Stacey, you have a new little cousin. She's as perfect as a baby can be, but just a wee bit smaller. Like a little angel."

"What's her name?" asked Mac.

"We don't know yet. Your mom and dad haven't decided."

"Maybe we could help pick one." Jon jumped up and down. "Like…maybe…Betsy!"

While everyone laughed again, Abby saw excitement flash in Stacey's eyes. She watched her carefully and wondered what she'd say. She didn't have to wait long.

"I know a name," Stacey said in a confident voice. "It's the best name she could have."

All eyes were on Stacey now. Elinor's, Jon's, Mac's, Maureen's, Cindy's and Abby's. But Abby's mind also raced, and in a flash she knew what Stacey was about to say.

"I think the perfect name for our new angel baby," Stacey began, "would be...Claire."

The name resonated in the air, and everyone— even the boys—was silent. Elinor blinked rapidly but couldn't prevent a tear from falling. "From life to death to life again. The full cycle," she whispered, "but how does a nine-year-old know?"

Abby's smile wobbled as she walked to Stacey and embraced her. "I love your idea, sweetheart."

"And I love you, Abby."

Whoosh! "I'm honored," she whispered. Abby glanced up and found Elinor studying her and Stacey. For the first time since Abby had met her, Elinor looked concerned.

THE REST OF THE WEEK seemed to pass in an instant. Between the busy orchard, the family and Jake, Abby barely had a minute to think. All too soon,

Jake was back in Boston, his vacation over, and Abby missed him five minutes after he left.

She waited for the school bus with the children on that first Monday of October and then drove slowly back, enjoying the memories of the past week. No matter what the activities during the day, she'd spent every evening with Jake. Often Stacey would accompany them on long walks, but after she'd been tucked into bed, Abby and Jake had had time for themselves. Nights making long leisurely love or hot passionate love; nights spent exploring the possibilities of love.

Now Abby parked her car and walked into the kitchen of the big house to find Susan sitting at the table, coffee in hand. She smiled at her.

"I want to thank you, Abby," said Susan. "We could never have handled everything here without you. Knowing you were in charge of the children gave me peace of mind while I was away. And the house is spotless."

"You can thank Jake for that, not me," Abby replied as she poured herself some coffee. "He came through with the cleaning service for as long as you want it."

"Foolish man," Susan said with a grin. "Does he think I'll ever stop it? I love being spoiled."

"Spoiled? Susan, you are far from spoiled. All Jake wants is for you to rest and recover and take care of yourself. He's happy to provide the help."

Tears suddenly rolled down Susan's face. "I'm so lucky," she gulped. "Everyone is so kind."

Stunned at the complete change in her demeanor, Abby quickly handed Susan a tissue and reminded herself about wacky hormones in postpartum women. "You and Rob have been kind, also," said Abby, trying to divert Susan's thoughts. "Stacey is thrilled that you named the baby Claire."

Susan's grin emerged again. "Oh, that wasn't kindness on my part," she said. "It was for my daughter's sake."

"Your daughter's sake?" Abby questioned. "What do you mean?"

Susan leaned toward Abby, and started to whisper. "Rob might have gone for Courtland, or Delicious, or who knows what!"

Abby burst out laughing, then giggled. "It might have been even worse," she said. "How about Granny Smith?"

Now Susan whooped. "A baby called Granny!" She dabbed the tissue to her streaming eyes while holding her stomach. "Oh, God, I'm hurting all over but I can't stop laughing."

Abby leaned back in her chair, enjoying the foolish conversation, the mirth and camaraderie. "No matter what your reasons, my friend, Claire Rose is a beautiful name."

"And so is Abigail MacKenzie," replied Susan.

"What?" Abby answered with surprise.

"You're a beautiful person, Abby. You've changed the lives of two people I love, and I hope…I hope very much…that…"

Abby held her hand up. "Don't say it, Sue. I know what you're thinking, but I'm not ready. I'm still working things out."

"Then take your time," replied Susan. "True happiness is worth the wait."

BY WEDNESDAY NIGHT, Abby felt that Jake had been away forever. By Friday night, she was as anxious as Stacey to see the man. It was ridiculous! But as she watched Stacey anticipate her dad's arrival, she started to understand the myriad emotions that the child experienced every single week as Friday night approached.

After dinner, Abby stood inside the front screen door, while Stacey sat with Betsy on the steps of the porch. She waited quietly, wanting to observe the greeting between father and daughter to see if Jake's observation was correct. Did Stacey hold back when she saw him?

Betsy sat at attention, ears straight up, focused on the road. She barked before Abby had any inkling that Jake's car was approaching. But then she spotted the headlights, and her own heartbeat increased to a gallop. She watched as Jake parked and strode toward his daughter. Stacey stood up and waited. Then she tilted her head, studied Jake, and walked slowly toward him. Jake picked her up, swung her around and she clung to his shoulders. Finally, a smile crossed the girl's face, and Abby concluded that Jake was on target. His daughter's tentativeness with him was apparent. Her inner conflict had not disappeared.

Stacey lifted a hand and pointed at the door. Jake looked up, smiled, and without taking his eyes from Abby, carefully placed Stacey on the ground and walked toward her. She opened the screen door, stepped into his arms and knew she didn't want to be anywhere else.

"I never knew a week could be so long," whispered Jake between kisses.

"Neither did I," admitted Abby.

He gave her another kiss, then reached for Stacey's hand. "Let's go inside, ladies. I've got some news. Seems this is going to be my year."

More professional success? Abby glanced at Jake, admiring his self-confidence, envying his eagerness to take on additional work. She was still nowhere near ready to resume her full-time practice. Fortunately, Martin hadn't asked, even once, if she was ready to come back.

They walked down the hall to the kitchen where Jake began to speak.

"I've been invited to be on a panel at the national cardiology conference next month. It's an annual event and, to be truthful, I'm a last-minute substitute, but what the heck? I've been asked and I'm going to do it.''

"Of course you should," said Abby, catching some of his excitement. "No question about it. I think it's wonderful."

"More wonderful than you know, because it's in Los Angeles." Jake swooped down and kissed Abby again. "Come with me, Abby. We'll fly there, and you can show me your hometown."

Los Angeles? Next month? "But my leave of absence will be up," she protested. "I'd be returning to L.A. anyway."

Jake's stunned expression reflected his disappointment and she was sorry she'd protested.

"Forget the sabbatical," he replied. "Just come with me for fun. For a visit. Be a tourist for a long weekend." His eyes implored.

It made sense. Every word of it. But her stomach knotted anyway.

"Can I come, Daddy?" asked Stacey, hope written all over her young face. "I want to go with you and Abby to California. I've never been there."

"You'll miss a day or two of school," Jake warned.

"Oh, pooh. That's nothing. I can make up the work."

"All right, then. If Abby gives the okay, we'll all go together."

Abby followed the conversation between father

and daughter, slightly numb as the implications hit her. Jake and Stacey in California meant introductions to her family, handling her mom's questions and expectations, and facing her career. Oh, Lord. She wasn't ready. But when she looked into Jake's and Stacey's anxious faces, she smiled and nodded. They'd be going to California…together.

THE APPLE HARVEST SEASON drew to a close at the end of October. Abby said goodbye to Lucy and the other friends she had made, many of whom promised to come back next year. Permanent staff remained, however, as part of the year-round retail operation involved in sorting, grading and shipping apples to supermarkets. Robert's job now was to get the orchard ready for winter. Equipment storage, mowing and tree pruning had to be supervised.

"So you don't run to Florida during the cold weather, huh?" Abby teased during brunch on the last Sunday of the month.

"Not quite," laughed Robert. "There's enough work for me on these acres for every season of the year."

"Then let's leave him to it," said Jake. "We've got errands to run before we finally see the famous or infamous Maureen Cooper starring in *Hello, Dolly!*"

Abby batted him with a fork. "Watch it, buddy. That's my aunt you're slandering."

Elinor had been at the opening-night performance the evening before, part of a group of Maureen's friends, and Abby had prepared to go as well. Maureen, however, had insisted that she, Jake and Stacey attend the matinee performance today. And Jake suggested that, before the show, they do some shopping for Abby.

"I won't have you freezing to death in your sunny-California clothes," he'd said yesterday. "The days are getting frosty. Time to get a heavy jacket and wool pants and some sweaters and stuff." Suddenly he looked confused. "Hmm…we'll figure it out when we get there."

Now, as they walked to the car, the sun shone and the outdoor temperature was almost as warm as any typical summer day.

"This is nuts," said Abby. "Why am I buying woolens when the weather's changed again?"

"Because it won't stay this way," responded Jake. "Just because we've got a beautiful day, doesn't mean we won't freeze tomorrow." He tipped his head and studied the sky. "The air is still, and there's some haze over to the west," he said. "We might get rain later on. So let's enjoy the sunshine while we've got it."

"No argument here," said Abby. "Come on, Stace. Into the car."

Stacey hopped in the back, wearing a plaid jumper and a long-sleeve turtleneck. She automatically belted herself into the middle seat. "Can we buy Aunt Maureen a bouquet of flowers and give them to her at the end of the show? I saw that on television once. It was for a singer. She was bowing and bowing and she got lots of flowers. Do you think Aunt Maureen will bow a lot?"

"Flowers are a great idea!" said Abby. "And yes, I do think Aunt Mo will bow for as long as people are applauding. My aunt's a ham. She likes to perform and get the attention."

Stacey giggled. "Then I used to be a ham, too. Remember, Daddy when I was little?"

Abby glanced at Jake. Alertness showed in every feature. He slowed the car, turned his head slightly and smiled at his daughter.

"I remember a lot of things when you were little, Pumpkin."

"I remember people clapping for me."

"What a good memory you have! How come they were clapping for you?"

Stacey turned her head and stared out the window. "I don't remember."

Jake reached a hand behind him between the split seats and patted Stacey's knee before accelerating the car once again. "That's okay. Maybe you'll remember later. In the meantime, we'll clap for Aunt Mo."

FOUR HOURS LATER, after Stacey presented the flowers and they'd visited a triumphant Maureen backstage, Abby, Jake and Stacey walked through the small lobby of the community theater toward the exit. Abby could barely see beyond the glass doors. She glanced at her watch. It was still late afternoon.

"My goodness. What happened out there? It's as dark as night."

Jake pushed at the door with difficulty. "The wind's tearing across the sky and it's raining hard. You two stay here, while I bring the car around."

Abby watched Jake sprint across the parking lot, until he was lost in shadow.

"I don't like storms," said Stacey, stepping closer to Abby.

"Lots of people don't, sweetheart," Abby replied, hugging the child to her. "But storms pass by, and the sun comes out again. I just can't believe how quickly the weather changed today."

Stacey looked up at her then. "Around here, people say, 'If you don't like the weather, wait five minutes.' That's what they say."

"Well, I guess they're right," Abby replied with a smile. "And look, Dad's here. Let's go."

She leaned against the door, and almost stumbled when the wind whipped it wide-open. She grabbed Stacey's arm and together they battled the gusts to the car, and finally were safely inside.

Lightning crackled, illuminating the area for a moment. Abby scanned the scene. Trees bowed in the wind, leaves and twigs skittered across the ground. Other theatergoers struggled to their vehicles.

"It's a good day to be home," said Abby.

"And that's just where we're going," replied Jake. "Is everyone strapped in?" He turned around. "Show me, Stacey."

Stacey pulled on her belt. "I know how to close it, Daddy," she said, exasperation in every word. "I'm not a baby!"

"How about you?" he asked Abby.

"I know how to close it, Jakey," replied Abby in Stacey's cadence.

The child giggled. Jake squeezed Abby's hand and whispered, "Smart aleck." Then he put the car in motion.

STACEY SAT BACK in her seat. She loved being together with her dad and Abby. She wished the storm hadn't come, but she'd enjoyed the day. And she had a friend in school. And a new baby cousin who was a girl. Now they'd be even at home. Two boys and two girls. Yes. Life had gotten better since Abby came.

Lightning cracked again and she jumped in her seat. Ooh, she really hated storms. She looked out the side windows and saw sheets of rain coming down. Then she looked at the front windshield. Wet leaves hung on to the wipers as they moved across the glass.

Thunder boomed; her heart boomed, too. She wrapped her arms around her stomach. Another crack of lightning, another roar of thunder. Stacey closed her eyes and heard herself moan. Suddenly, the car swerved hard.

"Oh, oh!" she cried, keeping her eyes shut.

"We're fine, Stace." Daddy's voice. "Everything's under control."

She breathed. She felt the car roll forward again and opened her eyes. The wipers still swished furiously, the rain continued to pelt them. Wet leaves flew at the windshield.

Just like snow. Thick. Fast.

No, no! No more.

Suddenly, the car spun around. She heard a familiar voice yell, "Hang on, hang on, honey."

"I am, Mommy," Stacey cried. "I am." Then, she screamed. "Look, look! Look at the truck. It's coming at us. The truck! Drive away, Mommy. Drive! Drive!... Please drive..."

"I'm trying," her mom cried, "but it won't turn...we're in a skid... Oh, my God... No!... No!... Sta—c-e-y!..." Her name echoed through the car until...

Crash! Stacey felt herself fly as far forward as the seat belt allowed and then fall back.

"I'm sorry, Mommy," she sobbed. "I'm sorry.

It's all my fault. My fault. I made you drive." She shook her head from side to side. "Wake up, Mommy. Please wake up. I can't reach you and I'm afraid. Please, please wake up. I can't move. I can't open the stupid belt. Where is everybody? I want my mommy!"

Finally, finally, she felt someone next to her. A woman. Soft. A woman was kissing her on the head, on the cheek. "I'm here, Stacey. I'm here. Don't be afraid."

Stacey reached with both arms. "I'm sorry, Mommy."

"It's not your fault, sweetheart. You didn't make me drive."

"But it was the rehearsal for my recital. And I wanted to go. And I kept begging you."

"But I wanted to go, too. So I decided to drive. Me, not you."

Her mom pulled her onto her lap and Stacey lay against her chest. "Remember, Stacey. The accident was not your fault. And that's the truth. Mommies don't lie."

"But..."

"But what?"

"But Daddy thinks it's my fault."

"He does?"

"Yes," said Stacey. "That's why he stays alone in the apartment. He doesn't want me. That's why I live with Grandma. Maybe some Friday night he won't even come back to the orchard."

Her mom hugged her tighter and it felt so good. "I promise you, Stacey, that you're wrong about that. Your daddy loves you more than he loves anyone else in the world."

"I don't think so."

"Then there's only one thing to do. We're going to ask him."

"Ask him?" Stacey's breath caught. "But what if he says it's true. He doesn't want me anymore?" A sob escaped as she exhaled.

"Listen to me, sweetheart. I promise you're going to get the answer you want. And then you can stop worrying, and your bellyaches will go away."

Stacey shrugged her shoulders. Maybe it didn't matter anymore. One way or another, anything was better than living with all the worry and pain.

"I'm going to rub your back, Stacey, gently up and down. And as I do that, you're going to start waking up. You've been sleeping for a while, and now it's time to get up." The voice was soft and low. It sounded familiar, but it wasn't her mom's.

Stacey opened her eyes. She was in the back seat of the car, but not in her belt. Instead, she was on Abby's lap and her dad was sitting next to them, tears trickling down his face.

"What happened, Daddy? Why're you crying?"

She sat straight and looked around her. Something terrible must have happened. Daddy never cried.

He wiped his eyes. "We skidded on a mess of wet leaves and had a little accident. Nothing to worry about, Pumpkin."

"An accident?" She started to cry. "But it's not my fault. It's not my fault. Mommy said it wasn't."

"Of course it isn't, Pumpkin," said Jake. "Accidents don't happen on purpose, that's why they're called accidents. They're not anybody's fault. And certainly not your fault. Not this one and not when Mommy died. Get it?"

Yeah. She got that much. But…but… "But you know what else?" Her tears came pouring out again, but she made herself look at her dad.

"What, sweetie. What else? Tell me everything."

She would. This time she would. "Mommy went to heaven," she gulped. "But I was in the car, too, and I stayed here! Why did I live and she didn't? It's not fair."

Her dad scooped her up from Abby's lap and kissed her all over.

"I give thanks every day that you lived. That you're here with me. I love you with all my heart, Pumpkin."

She leaned into his chest. Her daddy really loved her. He didn't blame her for the accident. He was big and strong and now she could feel safe.

"I still wonder if I could have changed things that

day,'' said Jake. ''Maybe if I had been behind the wheel, the accident wouldn't have happened. I was more used to driving in snow. I should have spent more time showing your mom how to drive in winter weather. But I didn't. I meant to, but I was so busy at work I kept putting it off. So if you want to blame anyone, you can blame me.''

Stacey thought about it for a minute, then looked outside. ''I don't blame you, Daddy,'' she said. ''But you got us into *this* accident. Maybe *you* need driving lessons!''

Her dad started to laugh even though his eyes looked teary, and Abby joined in. They laughed for a long time and it almost sounded like music when they laughed together. Finally, Stacey felt a grin start to spread across her own face.

She closed her eyes and leaned against her dad. She felt so good. Nothing hurt. There was just one more thing that would make life perfect. She opened her lids and looked from her dad to Abby and back to Jake again. If only... If only...they could be a family.

CHAPTER FOURTEEN

ABBY TOSSED her small suitcase on the bed and began packing for the flight to Los Angeles. She still wasn't sure why she was going, but at least her wardrobe would be appropriate for California weather.

Her thoughts wandered to her traveling companions. It seemed they were always on her mind. She'd finally admitted to herself that she'd done a good job helping Stacey and that the pleasure she felt was deserved. Surely she'd taken a step, albeit a small one, toward reclaiming her own self-confidence. But Abby still felt intimidated about committing to her practice in California, and she wasn't ready to commit to Jake in Massachusetts. Not while she still suffered the horror of finding a blood-soaked Tom Conroy in her office as she'd done again last night.

So her personal nightmare wasn't over. Maybe it never would be. Maybe she'd never again be the eager, confident woman she'd been before the tragedy, doing work she believed in.

Abby bit her lip as she continued packing. Sure,

Jake had been there for her last night, calming her down, wiping the sweat and tears from her body, but a frightened Abby wasn't the real Abby! And it wasn't the Abby she wanted to bring into a relationship.

"Why does nothing come easily?" she whispered, thinking of Jake, of the concern etched on his face as he comforted her, of the love shining in his eyes, and of his desire to get married. She closed the top of her valise and locked it, then—still thinking of Jake—automatically checked the room for anything she might have missed.

Married? No way. Not now. Not when she still had her own issues, and not when Jake was so damn grateful to her for Stacey's improvement, he'd be willing to do anything.

Abby bit her lip and wheeled her suitcase to the door. Why wasn't she happier with her decision?

"Isn't this great?" asked Stacey for the tenth time as she bounced in her window seat on the plane. "You can almost touch the clouds, and look how small the cars are and the roads."

"Look hard, Pumpkin. Soon we'll be flying over the clouds and you won't see anything down below," replied Jake. He turned to grin at Abby and shook his head.

She knew what he was thinking, and she agreed. The two weeks since Maureen's show and the accident in the rain had been incredible. Stacey had been incredible. In Jake's words, "She had come back to life." Now, happy and vivacious, she danced around the house while singing to herself or listening to the radio or playing cassettes. Her stomach-aches were virtually gone. In essence, she acted like a normal nine-year-old girl.

But most satisfying to Jake, Abby knew, was the greeting he got from Stacey when he returned to the orchard on Friday evenings. The child absolutely flew into his arms.

Jake's wish had come true.

"Can I ever thank you enough for this miracle, Abby?" he asked while fastening his seat belt on the plane.

Shoot. Not again. "You *have* thanked me enough, and frankly, Jake, I don't want to hear it even one more time." She heard her strident tone and winced.

His grin faded along with the twinkle in his eye.

"What's wrong, sweetheart?"

"Please don't thank me anymore. Helping people like Stacey is what I do for a living," she replied. "Post-traumatic stress disorder. PTSD. That's what I deal with and that's what Stacey was suffering from. I helped her. You helped her. And now she's better. And that's the end of our story."

He studied her face until she became uncomfortable.

"Clarify that last statement for me, please," he

finally asked, his eyes narrowing. "I don't want any misunderstandings. What do you mean, 'end of our story'? End of whose story?"

His eyes bored into her, his body didn't move. Abby doubted he breathed. He could have been a statue carved of stone. She knew what he was asking, what he wanted to hear, and she knew her words would hurt him. Dear Lord, she would be hurting the man she loved.

She forced herself to maintain eye contact, when all she wanted to do was hide under the seat. "I just don't know, Jake. I'm sorry, but I don't know the end of our story."

ABBY MAY HAVE BEEN CONFUSED an hour earlier, but Jake wasn't. He'd leaned over and kissed her after hearing the words that almost brought his world to an end. When her mouth softened within seconds, he knew all he needed to. He loved her with everything he had. And underneath all her fears, she loved him, too.

Returning to Los Angeles, to her family, to her colleagues, to her office definitely contributed to her doubts. She was coming home while her fears still haunted her, and everyone important in her life would know. All she needed was more time and more talks with Dr. Bernstein. No apologies were necessary. Not in his mind.

Now he glanced over at the two sleeping females

in his life and his heart expanded. He loved them both and they loved each other. He'd make it work, no matter what he had to do.

Then he turned back to his notes. His panel was presenting tomorrow morning and he had to be sharp despite the little sleep he'd get that night.

Ninety minutes later, they began their descent into the Los Angeles area. Jake checked his watch. It would be ten o'clock by the time they reached their hotel, but it would be one o'clock in the morning for them. Jake shrugged. Still time for a half-night's sleep. It would be enough, and if not, he'd make a damn fool of himself in front of the best and the brightest in American cardiology.

AFTER TAKING ADVANTAGE of the valet parking service for their rental car, Abby walked through the revolving door of the Los Angeles Hilton and stepped into the vast lobby. She turned and waited for Jake and Stacey to follow her. When she looked around again, she had to blink twice. "Oh, my. Look who's here."

"Who?" asked Stacey, letting go of Jake's hand and skipping closer to Abby.

But Abby's eyes were glued to three six-footers and one brown-eyed lady all walking toward them. "Stay with Daddy, Stace," she ordered as she flew into her mother's arms. And then her father's, where she was swallowed up and twirled around.

"Stop, Dad! I'm too big for you to do that," she protested with a laugh. She looked from one parent to the other, with lips trembling. "You're both a sight for sore eyes, I'm thinking," she said with a brogue in her voice and a tear in her eye. "And my brothers, too. Kevin and Sean." She reached up to kiss each of them. "But why are you all here? I gave you my flight number, but I didn't expect you here at the hotel."

In truth, she knew the answer. She looked at each of them, each one of her family who'd come to surround her with their love and protection. Her mother, whose eyes never stopped roving over her from head to toe, making murmuring noises about how much better she looked. Her dad, who studied her face. "I'm fine," she reassured him. And her brothers, who...who were examining Jake with piercing eyes.

Kevin walked over to her. "Come here a minute." He took her arm and led her away. "Just wanted to let you know, we checked him out."

"Who? What?"

Her brother's mouth tightened.

"You mean Jake? You checked out one of the finest doctors in the country?" She couldn't believe it, but she might have known.

"He's clean," continued Kevin as though she'd never interrupted.

What a surprise.

"Checked out his whole family, too. They're okay."

She winced with the knowledge that her good friends at the orchard had been under scrutiny because of her.

"Why do you do these things, Kev, without asking me? I'm a big girl now. I can take care of myself."

"Hey, don't blame just me. We were all in it together, Dad, Sean and I. And I don't see what's so bad. You weren't exactly in great shape when you left. We've had a hell of a time worrying about you. The old man, especially."

"But I called every week."

"Calls mean squat around here when people are worried. The folks needed to see you. Hell, Sean and I almost flew East last month, just to check up on you, but Mom stopped us."

Abby couldn't hide her surprise. "She never said a word to me on the phone. Did our easygoing mother really stop the MacKenzie men from doing what they wanted? It's hard to believe."

"Are you kidding?" said Kevin. "She was a tiger. 'My daughter is a strong woman who can take care of herself,'" he mimicked. Then he held her by the shoulders. "So, tell me, Abby, my strong sister. Was she right?"

Abby lifted her chin. Whatever her own doubts about her recovery and her relationship with Jake, she'd work them out herself, not in front of an audience. "Of course she was right," she responded. "I'm strong. I'm invincible, just like the song says."

Before Kevin could continue his interrogation, she heard Stacey's sweet voice.

"That lady looks just like Aunt Mo, doesn't she, Daddy?"

"That's because Maureen is my sister," Doris MacKenzie answered Stacey's question.

Stacey's blue eyes widened. "She is? Wow! Do you sing and dance, too? Aunt Mo is real good. She was in *Hello, Dolly!* and she was Dolly. Everybody clapped for a long time."

Doris laughed. "We used to sing duets, but Maureen is the star of the family."

"Abby can do stuff, too," said Stacey with enthusiasm. "She's great. We dance together. And Abby's really good at aerobics. We do them all the time. Together. Abby's my partner."

"I see," said Doris, glancing at her daughter.

Abby had no trouble reading her mother's expression. Stacey was staking her claim. No surprise there. The child was bright and sensitive, and wanted everyone to know that Abby was hers.

She had no trouble reading Jake's expression either. The man knew exactly what was going on.

"Why don't Stacey and I give you folks some time to visit?" he asked. "We'll take the bags upstairs. It's Room 716, Abby. Here's your key. If we're not back down in ten minutes, you'll know Stacey fell asleep.''

Abby chuckled silently. Jake lost no time staking his own claim, either.

"But I'm not tired, Daddy," said Stacey with a yawn. "I slept on the plane."

"Say good-night to everyone, just in case," said Jake, taking Stacey by the hand.

"Okay," she replied, covering another yawn. "Good night, everybody, and Aunt Mo's sister."

"Good night, darling," said Doris. "You can call me Aunt Doris for now. How's that?"

"Good."

Abby watched Stacey and Jake disappear into the elevator with the bellhop. When the door closed, she smiled at her family and led them to a quiet corner.

"He's a wonderful man," she began. "A terrific father and an esteemed physician. And I love him."

Her mom smiled; her dad waited.

"But I'm not sure he loves me."

"What?" they both responded.

She held up her hand. "You don't understand. He *thinks* he loves me, but…I think he's confusing gratitude with love." She looked at each in turn. "In a way, I saved his daughter's life…and…now I just don't know."

"Well, how did he feel before Stacey's recovery?" asked her mom.

Abby thought back. "There was love…lots of

love. Oh, just forget it! I'm too sensitive. That's all. Jake's a wonderful guy.''

"Sweetheart, what can we do to help?" asked Doris.

"Nothing. I'll work it out."

"There's nothing to work out," said Patrick. "What there is, is too much mumbo jumbo. Either he loves you or he doesn't love you. If he loves you, fine. If he doesn't, you don't need him. Period. Finished. Zero.''

If the world were as simple as Patrick wanted it to be! Abby looked at her family and loved them all. Just for caring and loving her. And for believing in her.

"We'll come for dinner tomorrow night," she promised. "Jake, Stacey and I.''

AFTER BREAKFAST the next morning, Abby, with Stacey in tow, collected the car and drove to her apartment. Three months earlier, she'd had high hopes that when she returned she'd be totally over the trauma. Evidently, it was not to be.

She opened the door to her home and walked in. So familiar and yet so strange. So small! Her hiatus in the country, living next to open fields and space, made her apartment seem minuscule even when compared to her cottage. She checked her thoughts. She'd had no complaints about the place before her trip and she could get used to it again.

She spent a minute running water in the sinks and flushing the toilet. Dust had accumulated on the hardwood furniture, and she dug out a cloth to use for polishing.

"Can I help?" asked Stacey.

Abby threw her another rag.

"You know, I used to live in an apartment, too. The one where Daddy lives now," said Stacey.

"I know," replied Abby.

"He says Betsy wouldn't be happy there."

"He does say that."

"I think she would," said Stacey.

"Really?" Abby smiled and waited. Where was Stacey going with this conversation?

"He says that I wouldn't be happy there."

"Uh-huh," Abby murmured.

"But I think I would. Just like Betsy."

"Okay. Tell me why."

"I think that people who love each other should live together. Don't you?"

"You know what I think?" Abby asked.

"What?"

"I think you should tell Daddy how you feel. He would want to know. You guys have no secrets anymore, right?"

"Right. And Abby?"

"What?"

"This apartment is too lonely. I'm glad you're coming home with us."

"Come here, funny-face, and put this in your memory. I love you, no matter what. For always and forever."

Stacey clung to her. "And me, too, no matter what, Abby. For always and forever."

"Good. So let's finish up and I'll show you the Pacific Ocean until it's time to go to see my friend, Dr. Bernstein, this afternoon. Your daddy will meet us there."

IF HER APARTMENT provoked little emotion, the mental health clinic more than made up for the lack. Abby cursed under her breath as she pulled into her familiar space in the garage, near the entrance to the building. She wiped her moist hands against her slacks and wondered how often she'd repeat the action before the day was done. Pasting a smile on her face, she turned to her companion. "Come on, Stacey. Let's go."

She led the child down the corridor, turned right and opened the door to the suite. Her hand slipped on the knob. Sucking in air, she paused on the threshold and looked around with such intensity that Stacey's chatter faded into the distance.

In the comfortable room, lush floor plants stood among the chairs and sofas, providing an illusion of privacy. Stacks of magazines covered several tables, and built into the wall opposite the entrance, a giant fish tank housed small schools of colorful tropical species.

Nothing had changed.

She glanced toward the corridor where her office was located and quickly averted her gaze. Visiting Martin today was probably a mistake. She was not ready—this was not the homecoming she'd imagined.

She took a deep breath and stepped across the floor to the reception area, Stacey at her side.

"Abby! Welcome back." The receptionist's green eyes sparkled with warmth as she greeted Abby, and for the first time since she'd entered the parking garage, Abby felt herself relax.

"Hi, Sharon. How are you?"

"Just great. Wondering when our most popular therapist was returning."

Heat traveled to Abby's face. "Please," she said. "No compliments. Is Dr. Bernstein ready to see me?"

The young woman stared at her and reached for the phone. "Let me check!" She glanced at her watch. "You're a little early, but…"

"Don't interrupt him, Sharon. We'll wait." Abby looked around again, her eyes once more darting toward her old office. She nodded in its direction. "Anyone in there?"

Sharon shook her head. "That's all yours, Abby. Everything in place. Just as you left it."

Abby closed her eyes for a moment, hoping Sharon was wrong. The last time she'd seen her office... She wouldn't go down that road. Instead, she turned to the receptionist. "Will you keep an eye on Stacey while I take a look?"

"Sure."

"Thanks." Abby smiled at the other woman and cautioned Stacey to keep an eye out for Jake and stay near the reception desk.

Then she straightened her shoulders and walked toward her office.

Dr. Abigail MacKenzie. The nameplate on the door welcomed her back. She gently touched her fingers to it. "That's me," she whispered before turning the doorknob.

Inside, the walls were freshly painted. All four of them plus the ceiling had been coated with a soft blue color easy on the eyes. And a deeper blue carpet had been recently laid, the distinctive new smell still lingering in the air.

Her gaze roamed to her desk. Framed pictures and diplomas lay stacked there. She slowly walked to them and stroked the clean glass protecting one of her diplomas. No one had rehung the items, but, like the walls, they were clean now.

Abby bowed her head, placed her hands on the desk for support and inhaled deeply. Then exhaled. Inhaled again. Exhaled again. Good. She was okay. She could rehang her diplomas where they belonged.

She could return to her practice if she wanted to. Tom Conroy wouldn't be haunting her anymore. It was over.

She whirled around, eager to share her news with Martin, then crashed to a stop.

Impossible! The walls had been clean a moment ago. "No," she whispered. "No more." She leaned back, her fingertips grasping the edge of the desk.

Red splotches covered the walls, pale *yellow* walls. Red splatters adorned plastic covers that hadn't been there a moment ago. And on the floor...she glanced quickly and moaned.

"No," she whispered. "Not again. Dear God, I can't go through this again, unless...unless...it *was* all my fault, wasn't it?"

Her eyelids closed. She felt tears run down her cheeks and thought her heart would rip into pieces as she stood there, in the place where her nightmare had begun. She'd been right all along. In the end, the fault was hers. No one else's. The fault was hers.

Breathing hurt. She couldn't move. Couldn't think of anything but Tom Conroy. Soon her lips started forming words, and like a mantra, she repeated, "It's all my fault." She said it once...twice...three times...until a second voice, a child's voice, joined hers in duet.

"It's all my fault. It's all my fault." The sweet voice of a girl...a girl she loved. Jake's daughter. The man she loved.

"No!" Abby shouted, stepping from the desk and shaking her fisted hands in the air. "I won't let this happen."

She turned, seeking, and Stacey's image shimmered before her. "No, Stacey, it wasn't your fault. And it's not mine either! Your dad tried to tell me. Martin tried to tell me. And they were right, I can't control everything. Or everyone. I can't make everything better."

She collapsed into the nearest chair, exhausted, but not finished. "There's still one thing I can do. Something that I've always done. I *can* help people *help themselves* to get better...*most* of the time."

She blinked her eyes, rubbed the tears away with the backs of her hands and scanned the room. The walls were clean. She was alone.

CHAPTER FIFTEEN

"WHAT'S ABBY DOING?" whispered Stacey as she and Jake peered into Abby's office. "She's just sitting there."

Good question. Jake stepped into the room, walked straight to Abby, and kissed her on the mouth. "Hi, sweetheart. What's wrong?"

"Hi, yourself. And nothing's wrong."

When she looked up, her smile dazzled him. Her eyes shone with a warmth that heated his blood, although traces of tears remained on her cheeks. Something had happened. Something had changed her. "What's going on?" he asked.

She rose from her chair and twined her arms around his neck. "A weight's been lifted," she replied. "I've found myself again and I'm feeling wonderful." Then she kissed him, which made him feel wonderful.

"Have you met with Dr. Bernstein already?" asked Jake when he caught his breath.

Abby paused, her forehead wrinkled. "Martin? No," she replied. "He didn't have anything to do with this at all, except…for having confidence in me.''

She flung her arm in an arc. "This is my office,'' she said. ''New paint, new carpet, just waiting for me.'' She looked into Jake's eyes. ''And I'm ready for it.''

His heart stopped. She wanted to stay here. In California. He studied her expression, her beautiful face. It was radiant and eager. She'd told him she'd needed to find herself. And now she had. Before him stood the person she'd been looking for. Before him stood the real Abby. And he loved her.

He stroked her cheek, cradled her face, and leaned in to kiss her. Sweet. Hot. Sizzling. Volcanic.

''Oh, wow! This is great. Keep it up.''

His daughter's voice finally penetrated his haze-fogged brain, and he pulled himself out of the kiss, but couldn't pull his eyes away from Abby. If he'd loved her before, he was crazy in love with her now and wanted her to be happy. He wanted all of them to be happy. And he knew how to make it happen.

He turned to his daughter. ''Stace, go watch the fish for a few minutes.''

''Just when it was getting good,'' his daughter complained as she dragged one foot behind the other on her way out the door.

He intercepted Abby's grin, and his confidence soared, but he wanted her full attention. ''Look this way, my love.''

And she did.

"You can have California if it's what you want," he whispered. "You've been through a tough time and if this is where you'll be happy, it's all right with me. In fact, I've already made a number of connections at the conference. With a little luck, I can probably network myself into a new hospital."

"What? I don't understand."

He kissed her again, and gently placed his hands on her shoulders. "I love you, Abby. I think about you day and night, every day and every night. And I will for the rest of my life."

He took a shaky breath, knowing his entire world hung in the balance of this conversation. "Marry me, Abby. I've asked you before, but maybe you weren't ready. So I'm asking again. Build a life with me. Through the good times, the bad times and all the times in between...."

Her eyes were bigger than the full moon in the night sky, her skin paler than milk. "You'd give up your job at Mass General?" she asked in a whisper. "You'd move here, to L.A.? For me?"

"I've been trying to tell you..."

She didn't give him a chance to tell her anything more. Instead, she wrapped her arms around him and started to cry. "I love you, Jake. Yes, yes, yes. I'll marry you."

His grin was tempered by her tears, but he managed another kiss before asking, "So why are you crying when you're supposed to be happy?"

She looked up at him through her lashes. "Because I thought you wanted to marry me only because I'd helped Stacey and that you were confusing the issues. But it wasn't you. It was me confusing everything. I'm so sorry."

"You thought I'd marry someone just for my daughter's sake?"

"So I'm an idiot!"

He grinned. "But you're my id... Nah..." He stopped himself. "The woman I love is definitely not an idiot. The woman I love is very wise and makes excellent decisions when asked important questions."

He kissed her again. He could have kissed her all evening right there in her freshly painted office, but people were waiting for them. "Let's go," he said.

But Abby went to her phone. "Sharon, can you bring Stacey back into my office?" she asked.

"Smart move," Jake admitted. "A little privacy before we meet your family for dinner."

"Exactly," she replied, stepping toward the door and opening it just as Stacey arrived. "Hi, sweetie."

"Hi. Are we ready to go?"

"In a minute," said Jake. "Abby and I have something to tell you."

"What?" asked Stacey, looking from one to the other as eagerness and anxiety battled for dominion in her voice and on her face. "Is it something bad or good?"

Jake glanced at Abby, surprised to see her biting her lip. She was nervous even though she knew Stacey was crazy about her. Well, maybe she had a right to be. This decision was real, not pretend. It was permanent, not temporary. The thought made him very content and he smiled.

"Come here, Pumpkin," Jake said, reaching for Stacey. He sat down and pulled her onto his lap. "I have good news. Very good news." Then he felt himself smile. Grin. He couldn't help it.

"What, Daddy?"

"Abby and I are..." He glanced at Abby, then back to Stacey. "Abby and I..."

"You're getting married!"

Jake nodded.

"That's so great." Stacey jumped from his lap and ran to Abby. He watched as his petite daughter almost knocked Abby to the floor with her enthusiastic hug. "I wished for this!" she gushed. "Daddy, you and me. Together for always."

Jake watched his two women in their embrace. Stacey rested against Abby with a comfort that bespoke trust. Life didn't get any better. Except, he still had to tell Stacey about moving to the West Coast. Not fair to trick her into a false happiness.

"There's more, Stace," he said. "Abby's a doctor, too, and her practice is here in California, her patients are here.''

"That's true," said Abby, "for the moment. But I'm beginning to wonder how living in Boston compares to living in Los Angeles, how treating members of Boston's Finest compares with treating members of the LAPD.''

What was she talking about? Didn't she want to remain in L.A.?

"I wouldn't want to be accused of stealing the most progressive cardiologist away from Mass General and the city of Boston," Abby continued. She looked at Jake and winked.

He felt his grin return. There was no one like Abby. No one else could come close.

"Maybe," Abby continued as she held Stacey's hands, "we could find a place big enough for all of us. You, Daddy, me and Betsy.''

"Oh, yes. That's exactly right," Stacey whispered before turning her shining eyes to Jake. "I want to be with you every night, Daddy, not just weekends. I want us to live together like other people do. And I was going to tell you that anyway because Abby said I should.''

How could he love a child as much as he loved Stacey and still have missed the point? But not anymore. "A house," Jake said. "We'll look for a house with a yard...a house big enough for a girl and her collie and two parents, and—'' he glanced at Abby ''—maybe a little extra room for the future.''

She met his glance and blushed; then she nodded. He loved it.

''And we can visit Grandma and everyone on the weekends,'' continued Stacey.

''And help with the harvest,'' said Abby.

Stacey ran to Jake holding her arms up. He hoisted her easily and reveled in the hugs she gave him.

''Daddy?'' Stacey whispered.

''What?''

''My heart's pumping a lot of love.''

''Mine is, too.'' He snuggled into her soft neck, bestowing kisses on every square inch of skin until he heard her giggle.

He looked at Abby. ''Come on over,'' he invited, holding out his arm. He tucked her against him, thankful for this wonderful woman and his second chance at love.

Abby peered up at him. ''Seems like you're pretty happy with yourself.''

''Sure am. I finally got smart. Smart enough to fall in love with you.'' He leaned down to kiss her. ''And smart enough to do something about it! I'm looking forward to a new beginning with the people I love.''

''A new beginning,'' Abby repeated, her voice lingering over the words.

"Absolutely," Jake whispered. "New beginnings for each of us individually and for all of us together."

Abby's eyes darkened with emotion, and then she smiled so sweetly he wanted to make love to her right there in her office.

"'All of us together.'" Abby repeated his words. "I like the sound of it. I like the feel of it. I like what it means. In fact, there's a name for what it means." She glanced at him with a raised eyebrow and challenge in her voice.

He grinned. If she thought he was afraid of the all-important word, she'd have to think again. "There sure is," he agreed. "One of the most important words in any language." He turned to look at Stacey, whom he still held in his arms. "Do you have any idea what we're talking about?"

Stacey's expression spoke volumes about how her dad was treating her like a baby, but then her big smile took over. "Of course I know. *Love.* You love Abby and me. Abby loves you and me. And I love both of you. We're going to be a *family!*"

"We sure are," said Abby. "Count on it."

Jake lowered Stacey to the floor, took Abby in his arms and kissed her with all the love in his heart. She was his future, and there was no one in the world like her. In the background, he heard his daughter cheering quietly.

Another perfect moment to savor. Reluctantly,

Jake ended the kiss and wrapped an arm around each of his women. "Come on, ladies. The MacKenzies are waiting, and we've got an announcement to make."

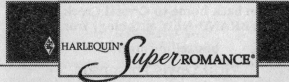

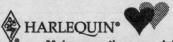

Princes...Princesses...
London Castles...New York Mansions...
To live the life of a royal!

**In 2002, Harlequin Books lets you escape to a
world of royalty with these royally themed titles:**

Celebrate a year of royalty with
Harlequin Books!

Available at your favorite retail outlet.